CHAPTER 1

I slammed my apartment door shut, nearly tripping over the stack of overdue bills on the floor as I made my way in. It was raining outside, and I was soaked through to the bone after waiting for the bus for over an hour.

Dropping my keys on the side, I kicked off my wet shoes and marched right over to the freezer, pulling out a microwave meal for one and slapping it down on the counter. I grabbed a fork out of the drawer and stabbed holes into the plastic film, taking the day's mounting frustration out on the helpless cellophane wrapper.

Packaging suitably abused, I slung the meal in the microwave, set the timer, and slammed the door closed. I zombie walked over to my couch and threw myself down, letting out a huge sigh.

From the apartment above came the distant thud of my neighbor, Jared, a self-professed 'DDR champion' that liked to practice at all hours of the night and day. After a long day of standing on my feet in the Craft Castle I just wanted a little peace and quiet. I groaned as the thudding became louder, pulled my phone out of my pocket, and texted him.

Dude, can you keep it down. I just got in.

A second later a message pinged back. *Sorry Zora no can do, I'm doing a twelve-hour charity stream!*

I let out another long sigh, picked up one of the couch cushions, and folded it over my head, attempting to wrap myself in a silent cocoon made of cotton and polyester. Rain sprinkled on my studio apartment window, a comforting sound even though the rain and I were not good friends at the moment.

'Studio Apartment' had a magical way of sounding glamorous until you actually saw one. It basically meant my entire life was crammed into one ugly little room. The only saving grace was a moderately sized window that looked over the city below, but for the most part my view was the roof of a neighboring apartment and an old alleyway where homeless people liked to hang out and do drugs.

City life wasn't quite as glamorous as TV had made it out to be.

When I first moved here things weren't so bad. I came here with my boyfriend, Tyler, who had been gifted a very generous deposit from his parents. We got ourselves a nice house in the suburbs and were ready to get started on the kids, the white picket fence, and the golden retriever… the whole shebang!

The dream hadn't lasted long however, and nowadays life felt more like a nightmare than anything else. It turned out Tyler was a serial cheater—but before that revelation the relationship already had plenty of red flags. He was controlling, psychologically abusive, and generally just made life unbearable.

I'd like to say I was better off now I was free—and I most definitely was—but Tyler was as cunning as he was despicable, and while we were together he'd taken out a bunch of loans and credit cards in my name, leaving me with an uncontrollable amount of debt. I took him to court, but the judge threw it out, claiming there wasn't enough evidence to prove Tyler had committed fraud in the first place.

So now I was stuck in this little box apartment, trying to make enough money to get back on my feet but making next to nothing at a craft superstore. It really did feel like I was scraping rock bottom, but to be honest, being at rock bottom right now would be a considerable upgrade from my current state.

CAKES TO DIE FOR

COMPASS COVE COZY MYSTERY BOOK 1

MARA WEBB

I just needed a break, a sign from the heavens, something to help pull me out of this slump. I sat up and stared at the rain-streaked window, urging the universe to give me anything. The microwave dinged and I jumped, forgetting I'd put it on in the first place.

"Looks like I'm not getting a break anytime soon," I muttered, standing up and heading over to get my dinner. I didn't even look to see what I grabbed out the freezer. I'd been rotating between lasagna, steak, and curry, but to be honest they all kind of tasted the same. I was halfway to the microwave when I heard a knock at the door.

Pausing, I turned toward the door and stared at it for a moment. I'd lost all my 'friends' when Tyler and I parted ways six months back, and I hadn't made any new friends since moving to this part of the city. No one ever knocked at my door, especially not this late at night.

Was this the saving grace I had been praying for?

I walked up to the door, looked through the peephole, and felt my hopes deflate as I saw the person standing on the other side. If I was quiet enough, I could just creep away from the door and pretend I wasn't in.

"Open up, Zora!" Mr. Andino shouted from the other side. He was my landlord, and I was considerably overdue on rent. It's not like I was spending my money on shoes and clothes; every spare dime I made went toward trying to pay off Tyler's debts. The collectors were not nice people, and they were starting to get really pushy. "I know you're in there, I saw you come in on the camera!"

"I'm sick," I lied. "I'm vomiting everywhere. Like *a lot*."

"Fine, you'll listen through the door then." As he said that I heard him push some paper under the door. "You have until Friday to pack up and leave. If you're not out by nine in the morning on Friday, the police will be here to help escort you off the premises."

"You're kicking me out?!" I said, panic starting to beat through me. "But you have to give me more than two days' notice!"

"I did. I told you four weeks ago you were on the last straw. You promised you'd get me the money, but typical Zora, that turned out to be a lie."

"I can pay. I just need a day to get the money, I can get you the rent!"

"No, time's up. I already have a new tenant for the space. Pack your things. Come Friday, you're gone."

Andino walked away without another word, leaving me on the other side of the door, the eviction notice clutched in my hands. I didn't bother reading through it; I already knew everything I needed to know.

"Take a breath, Zora," I told myself. "Let's get some food, and then make a plan. We can figure this out."

I headed back over to the couch, grabbing my microwave meal on the way. I didn't have money for cable or internet, so books were my main form of entertainment at the moment. I'd always been more of a reader anyway. With my TV dinner on my lap, I pecked at my microwaved gruel while reading my latest borrow from the library.

I'd barely taken two bites of my miserable red slush when another knock came at the door.

"Go away, Andino," I shouted. "You already made yourself clear!" Andino was a large Turkish man, and his default volume was loud. The walls and doors in this apartment block were so thin he'd definitely hear me from the hall, but he knocked again. "Seriously, dude?" I said. "I'm already having a bad day; a girl can't eat her microwaved-whatever in peace?"

Five more melodic knocks sounded on the door, and I put my food and book down on the floor. There wasn't room for a coffee table in this apartment, and even if there was, I couldn't afford one anyway.

With a huff I stomped back to the door, unlatched the chain, and threw it open. "What could possibly be so—oh." My anger dissipated as I saw that the person knocking on my door wasn't Andino. Standing there was a slender middle-aged woman in a long white coat, heels, and a small white clutch. Her hair was short and silver, and large black shades obscured her eyes. A string of plump white pearls hung from around her neck.

The first impression I got was 'money', and lots of it. This myste-

CAKES TO DIE FOR

rious woman didn't react much to me opening the door and screaming in her face, but she did raise one questioning brow.

"Having a bad day?" she asked, her voice amused and unwavering.

"Ever done a twelve-hour shift at the Craft Castle?" I asked.

"No, but I did a small stint in Vietnam." That took me by surprise. This regal-looking woman didn't strike me as the military type.

"Trust me, I'd take war over Craft Castle any day."

"You could always enlist," she suggested.

I pointed at the inch-thick glasses on my face. "Already tried. They're not interested in putting bottlecaps in boots."

One corner of her mouth lifted in a slight smile. "Just like Tabatha," she said cryptically. I had no idea what that was supposed to mean.

"Uh listen, you look like a very respectable person, and I'm sure whatever you're selling is great, but I've got no money, and I've got a pretty awful microwaved *something* going cold on the floor, so if you don't mind—" I went to close the door, but the woman put her hand out and stopped me.

"Actually, I was hoping I could come in."

It was more of a statement than a question, and it was said with such staunch self-belief that I found myself stepping back and letting this strange woman march into my apartment. I typically wasn't the type to shrink back, so I found myself perplexed at acting this way.

"Um, excuse me, but you're going to have to leave," I said as the woman walked into the one room that acted as my lounge, bedroom, and kitchen.

"My god," she said in marked disgust, taking her shades off to inspect my home. "I've seen prison cells with more room."

"It's cozy, but hey, I save on heating bills—" I stopped myself, wondering why I was still letting this stranger stand in my apartment, let alone belittle it. I marched over to the woman and stopped in front of her, staring for a second as I saw her eyes properly for the first time, bright blue, the same kind of crystalline azure you'd find on a white sand beach. "My goodness your eyes are so blue."

"A family trait," she said with a warm smile. "Now let's get down to—"

"You seem lovely and all, but it's time to go," I interrupted, taking the strange woman by the arm and shepherding her to the door. I pushed her out into the hallway. "Don't take it personally or anything, I'm sure whatever MLM you're peddling is great, but I've tried them all and they don't work, at least not for me! I'd love to chat, but I've got to pack and find somewhere new to live. Bye!"

I shut the door, bolted the chain, dropped my head against the frame, and let out a deep breath. There were lots of crazy people in this part of the city, and the only one that was allowed that far into my apartment was me.

Turning around to head back to my dinner, I let out a scream as I saw the woman somehow standing in my apartment again. "What in the?!" I screeched.

"Where were we? Ah yes, introductions. I'm Liza, Liza Thorn. You're—"

"I'm calling the police if you don't leave, *now*," I threatened. "Just how in the heck did you get back in here anyway? Are there two of you? Are you a twin?"

"Darling, the world can just about handle one of me. Now if we can get down to business, everything is—"

I pulled out a fire poker I had stashed near the front door for emergencies and brandished it in my hands as a weapon. "Okay, you've got until the count of three before I smack this thing around the side of your head."

"That's a little rash, don't you think? I just want to talk." The mysterious woman sat down on the couch and crossed her legs neatly. I found myself wondering what I had to do to intimidate this woman and get her out of my apartment.

"And I just want you to leave; now I'm perfectly within my rights to use this to defend myself," I said, holding up the fire poker like a baseball bat. I had to take a second glance at it then when the fire poker turned a different color and folded over in my hands. I was now holding a white silk scarf.

"What do you think?" the woman asked. I looked up and saw the scarf now folded around her neck. My hands were empty. "Too much with the coat, right?" She snapped her fingers and the scarf vanished.

"How in the—" I said, my mouth opening and closing again. "How did you do that?"

"Come and sit down, I promise I won't bite. Not with these dentures." The silver-haired stranger threw her head back and let out a hearty self-deprecating laugh. Seeing no other choice but to cooperate with this woman I cautiously made my way over to the couch and sat opposite from her, no longer concerned with my microwave food or book.

"Did I die? Am I having a stroke?" I asked. The bus could have crashed on the way back from the Craft Castle. Maybe I had a stress-induced aneurysm when Andino told me I was going to be homeless in two days. Heart disease was the world's biggest killer, and I was so badly addicted to sugar and everything else sweet that I was sure my old ticker wasn't long for this world.

"No, you're not having a stroke, but it *does* smell like a swimming pool in here," she said, wrinkling her nose and looking around the apartment in concern. "Is that chlorine?"

"It's the ventilation pipes outside, they're right under my window and—" I shook my head to stop myself getting sidetracked. "What is going on here? Is this some sort of MLM where you sell magic tricks? Because honestly, I'm kind of sold. Start me at the bottom, wherever you want; I'll peddle candles if you can teach me how you did that trick."

"That wasn't a trick, and I'm not selling anything," she said. "In fact, it's the opposite: I'm giving it away."

"I'm sure." I'd heard that classic line before. I'd sat through my fair share of marketing presentations just to get to the free buffet at the end. Hey, times are hard, and I've got about one hundred bucks left at the end of the month to make sure I don't starve to death; take your judgments elsewhere!

The regal-looking woman pulled a sealed wax envelope out of her thick white coat and handed it to me. The paper was crisp, slightly yellowed, and the blue seal on the back felt solid, with a large 'W' pressed into the set wax.

"What is this?" I asked.

"You're a witch, Zora, just like me. *Yes,* witches are *real.* That's how I did those unusual things just now." She snapped her fingers and a potted plant appeared in her palm. "We can conjure, manipulate, summon, unravel the very fibers of reality." As she said this, the plant turned into licorice, ignited in a dazzling pink fire, and burned until there were only a handful of shimmering motes left hanging in the air. I watched them curiously as they faded away one by one.

I looked down at the envelope in my hands. "And this?"

"That's your inheritance. You'll find an address inside. It's yours now. Make your way, it's time to start learning, you've got a lot to catch up on, and a lot of work to do!"

I lifted my eyes again to look back at the mysterious woman—or *Liza*, as she had introduced herself—and realized she was gone. I opened the envelope and found two things inside: a note with an address, and a folded map that seemed to show four towns around a large body of water. On the northern side of the water a town called 'Compass Cove' had been circled in red sharpie.

Underneath the address there was a short note written in elegant cursive handwriting.

See you there! –Liza.

CHAPTER 2

It seemed crazy, but with no other options left in life I figured it wouldn't hurt to bundle all my belongings together in the back of a crappy rental car and drive halfway across the country to take a chance on the mysterious ramblings of a complete stranger.

I spent the next two days packing up the things that were important—not much, mostly clothes and photographs of my dad—and scraping together the money for a rental to get me on the road.

My manager at the Craft Castle wasn't happy about me leaving without notice, but he was a misogynist pig anyhow and was overdue a little bad karma from the way he treated me and the others at the shop. I managed to sell a couple of knickknacks to scrape together the change for a car and ended up pulling out of the rental forecourt in a rust bucket that looked like it wouldn't make it much further than the state line.

The body of water on the map in my envelope was labeled 'Compass Cove' and after using the library Wi-Fi I located the town on the opposite coast, a mere forty-six-hour drive from Portland.

No biggie.

After four days of almost nonstop driving and coasting on fumes, I pulled into a town on the southside of Compass Cove, a little place called 'Sacketsville'. The engine of my rental spluttered to a stop in the forecourt of a gas station, completely emptied of gasoline and not moving another inch.

I got out of the car and headed into the shop, grabbing a bag of chips and an energy drink to keep me going. It was just after two in the afternoon, and after sleeping in Walmart parking lots for three nights in a row I was not feeling great.

"Looks like you rode in on the wind," a young woman remarked from behind the counter as I stepped up to pay.

"Me?" I asked, so delirious from sleep deprivation I couldn't hold a normal conversation.

"Yeah! I heard your car from up the street. You need gas in that bad boy, pronto!"

"Oh, well I literally have like three dollars left to my name, so I'm going to go for food and drink first."

The girl's mouth contorted in an unsure way, and she opened up the register. "Tell you what; the food, drink, and ten dollars of gas is on me."

I straightened up at her generosity. "Are you serious?"

"Sure! Hey, what's money for if you can't brighten someone's day every now and then?" she said with a wink. She pulled change out of her pocket and put it in the register.

I had to blink for a moment to try and compose myself. Typically, I wasn't a very emotional person, but I'd been having such a hard time recently and I can't remember the last time someone did something nice for me. "I think I could kiss you," I said. "Thank you so much."

"Eh, don't mention it. I'm trying to do that whole pay it forward thing? You know, you do something nice for someone, and the universe does something nice for you. My selflessness is totally selfish!" she said and winked. "I'm Ellie by the way. Have you been round here before? You look familiar."

"First time here," I said. "I—" I opened my mouth to recount the story about the strange woman in my apartment, but I stopped myself. How did I explain I'd driven halfway across the country on a complete whim? "Apparently I have family around here. I'm in town to meet up with a long-lost aunt."

Ellie stared at me for a moment, looking as though she was trying to place my face. "Your last name isn't Wick, is it?"

"How on earth could you know that?" I said with disbelief.

"Ah, I knew it!" Ellie said, her face lighting up in triumph. "You've got the look alright! Ooh boy, I didn't know they had more of you hidden out there. Who's your momma?"

"I uh—" I faltered; I'd spent my whole life wondering the same thing myself. "I never actually knew her. My dad raised me, though he passed a few years ago."

"Shucks, I'm sorry to hear that. Well welcome…"

"Zora," I said, realizing I hadn't given my name.

"Welcome to town, Zora. I hope you enjoy your stay here! Before you go let me get you one of these…" Ellie disappeared under the counter and then hopped up again a second later, holding a small vial on a key ring. "Take this," she said, handing it to me.

"Thanks?" I said with uncertainty, holding up the key ring and looking at it. There was a small hoop, and a chain that connected to a little glass tube no bigger than my thumb. Inside there was a tiny green plant with an orange bud on the end. "Uh… what is it?"

"A Thorn of St. Christopher. Keep it on you at all times and it will guarantee your safety. He's the patron saint of travel, and as you're traveling, I figured you could use some protection!"

"Thanks," I said again, hooking the key ring onto my purse. "Isn't St. Christopher usually on a small gold medallion?"

"That he is, there's a small one buried in the dirt inside the key chain. The medallions aren't much use by themselves though; you need a little botanical assistance to make sure he's keeping watch." Ellie winked and clicked her fingers at me. She seemed nice enough, but I also got the impression she was a little odd.

"I'll carry it until my dying day," I joked. "So anyway, I'm trying to get to the town on the north side of the water, I think it's called Compass Cove or something like that?"

"That's correct. I figured you'd be heading that way seeing as your family hales from there."

"You know a lot about my family?" I asked with surprise.

"Oh, everyone knows the Wicks around here," Ellie said in an indicative way. "They're well known to all locals!"

"Yikes, I'm not sure if that is in a good way or a bad way?"

"Eh… a little of Column A, a little of Column B," she said with an amiable smile.

"Right… well, looking at the map it seems like I can go either way around the water, is one way faster than the other?"

"They're about the same to be honest, but—Ah, I keep forgetting." Ellie's expression suddenly soured.

"What? What is it?" I asked.

"There was an earthquake here about a month back, it caused a few landslides around the cove. There's mountains on the north side, and both the roads going into Compass Cove town are washed out."

"You're kidding me!"

"Nope, they're trying to clear it up, but to be honest the cleanup is going slowly. There's a whole lot of dirt and rock on that road, and I think some of the road even got knocked into the water. It's going to be a while before the roads are open again."

"How am I supposed to get up there then?"

"Oh, you can use the water! Gordo's got a water taxi that can take you over. He's a good old egg, if you don't mind listening to the same three stories over and over again."

"Gordo?" I asked.

"Yeah, he's got a boat down on the pier, you can't miss him! In fact…" Ellie checked the time on her watch and twisted her face as though making a choice. "Ah, I can close for ten minutes and take you down there, help you find your way."

"You're sure? That's very generous of you. I don't want you getting in trouble."

"Trouble schmuble. The gas station belongs to my brother anyway; what's he going to do, fire his only sister? You're the second person I've seen today. Come on, let me take you down to Gordo."

Ellie led the way out of the shop, flipping the sign to closed and locking the door as we left. "You can leave your car here for now if you like, your things will be safe."

"It won't get stolen or broken into? All my things are in there."

"Nah, it's safe up here. Crime is next to nonexistent in these parts." Ellie eyed the car as we walked past, raising her brows at the pile of junk heaped onto the back seat. "Say, didn't they have a U-Haul near you or something? The car looks like it was packed by a Tetris grandmaster!"

I laughed. "Yeah, I'm a bit hard up on cash at the moment. To cut a long story short I wasted several years of my life on a guy and ended up with nothing aside from a whole lot of his debt."

"Financial or emotional?"

"Both," I chuckled glumly.

"His loss. Wick women are strong, and if he couldn't see that... too bad!" Ellie took a left onto a street that led down to the water. It was a gray day, overcast and a little cool, and as we got closer to the water the air felt cooler still.

Waves gently lapped against the sandy shore, and I followed Ellie onto a rickety old pier, at the end of which there was a cabin next to a boat in the water. The cabin was a small metal shack with a sliding window and a door. Ellie rapped her knuckles against the dirty glass while I stared at the green slime growing around the window frame.

An old man with a huge bushy white beard appeared out of nowhere and pulled the window back. "Eh?" he said.

"Gordo, this is Zora. She needs a ride to the other side of the water; can you help her out? She's a Wick."

Gordo's thick bushy white brows raised in intrigue. "Ah, came to replace Constance, did she?" Gordo's dusty green eyes flicked over to me. "Good luck!"

"Replace who?" I asked, just about making out the words over his thick seadog accent.

Ellie batted the question away with her hand. "Ignore him." She looked at the old sailor. "Stop making up gossip again. I already told you to write a book if you can't stop spinning yarns."

"Not spinning yarns," he mumbled. "Just seemed like a logical connection is all. Constance was the last one around this cove that tried to keep everyone happy."

I opened my mouth to question him, but Ellie got there first. "Can you run her across the water or not? Do it as a favor for me, your favorite granddaughter."

"Pah!" Gordo scoffed. "Coraline's my favorite, she brings me casserole every Friday, you just bring me grief!" He lumbered out of the old metal shack on bowed legs, each of his steps so rickety I was concerned he might fall. I had no idea how old this man was but he looked like he should have been in a retirement village instead of working on a boat. His back was so hunched he was almost bent over double, stooping so low he was shorter than Ellie and me.

"I can find another way across," I said to Ellie. "It's no trouble, really."

"I'm out of my chair now, you're going across that water, missy!" Gordo hollered. I held out my hand to help him make his way over to the boat, but he slapped it away. "Get out of here, I'm not some geriatric pity case!" Ellie just rolled her eyes.

There was a little ladder leading down from the jetty to a barnacle encrusted speedboat that also looked like it belonged in retirement. I almost couldn't bear to watch Gordo carefully turn around and navigate the ladder, and it turned out I didn't have to. In a surprising turn of events the old man hopped off the pier and landed in the boat gracefully, firing up the engine and dropping down into the seat like it was no effort at all.

He looked up at me and cackled. "Ha, ha! Got you, didn't I?!" Even his voice sounded less old now. I had fallen for his act hook, line, and sinker. I realized Gordo was now sitting up straight too, his hunch gone and his demeanor seeming decades younger.

"That's his idea of a good joke," Ellie explained, looking up at the skies in a way that suggested she had seen the 'joke' plenty of times before. "Be careful around that one; he might look old, but he's got more pranks up his sleeve than a bored schoolboy."

"Warning noted," I said as I climbed down the ladder and sat on the boat.

"Hey, what's a welcome party without a little fun?" Gordo said and winked at me as he untied the boat from the dock and waved at Ellie. He shouted after her as we pulled away. "I was just kidding; you are my favorite!"

"I already know!" she shouted while shrinking away into the distance. Gordo looked back at me and cackled again. Initially I had him down as ninety, but now he'd stopped the old man act I wasn't so sure. Maybe closer to sixty. He had a face that looked like it had been weathered by a lifetime of sea salt, so maybe he wasn't as old as he appeared.

"You could get an academy award with a performance like that," I said, breaking the silence that had come over the boat quickly after setting off.

"Probably could do," Gordo said and lit a pipe that had been stashed in a jacket pocket. "I don't really care for that kind of lifestyle though. Fast cars, big houses, grand pianos, monkey butlers. My best friend from when I was a boy became a famous actor you know."

"Oh?" I asked.

"You probably never heard of him, but he was a big film star back in the forties. Baxter Bluth."

I shook my head. "Can't say it rings a bell."

"We grew up as rural farm boys, but Baxter had a gift for physical comedy. Funniest guy I ever met. Well, he turned that trick to the trade, and before long his name was up in bright lights. Success came, and all the gilded trinkets that accompany it. They found him dead at thirty-seven, floating at the bottom of his swimming pool with a wheelbarrow of cocaine at the poolside."

"Are you kidding me?" I said, sitting back after realizing I had leaned in during the story.

"I swear on Theodore Roosevelt's cat. The police said he'd taken enough coke to down a grizzly bear, but the thing that had them really stumped was the orca whale floating in the pool too," Gordo stopped to take a puff and I found myself growing increasingly confused.

"An… orca whale?"

"Oh yeah! The police were just as confounded. They said, what's an orca whale doing in here? And the whale said, *'Hey, don't ask me, pal; I'm just here for the party!'*"

With that Gordo threw his head back and erupted in a fit of wild laughter, slapping a hand on his leg, his pipe in his mouth and his other hand on the rudder. It took me a second to realize I'd been had again.

"You never had a childhood friend called Baxter, did you?" I asked, a quick guardedness starting to develop for anything that came out of Gordo's mouth.

"Sure, I did, but he wasn't an actor. He moved to the city and became an eye doctor! Now *that's* a funny tale. He happened to be Mohammad Ali's optician. *That's* a true story. I bet you'd like to hear that."

I smiled and rolled my eyes, beginning to understand that Gordo was one of those mysterious types that got his entertainment from suckering others into believing his nonsense. "How far across the water do you get before people cotton onto your tricks?" I asked him.

"Well, put it this way, kiddo. I've lived here all my life and some people still haven't figured it out!" He threw his head back again and let out another bout of mad laughter. I found I couldn't help but smile a little at his infectious lunacy. "Ah, but you're one of those educated city types, eh? Can't put a trick past you it seems."

"Something tells me that's not going to stop you from trying," I said.

His eyes glistened with mischief. "Now there's a challenge I'll hold you to. Look alive, missy, Compass Cove town right ahead."

Turning around I saw the northern coast approaching. Gordo pulled the boat up to the pier, slung a rope over a post, and pulled us in close as he let the engine fall into idle. He hopped up onto the jetty and helped me out of the boat, not struggling at all as he hauled me up.

"Well, have a marvelous day," he said as he tapped his pipe ashes into the water. "I was actually heading over here myself. I've got a taxidermy moose head I need to pick up. I'm just hoping Madeline was able to fix up the saxophone."

"Sure, I'm sure all of that is completely true," I said, pressing my lips together in a tight smile and rolling my eyes. "Thanks for the ride, see you around."

"You know it!" he said, waving me off as I headed up the street leading into town.

CHAPTER 3

*A*t the water's edge there was a sand beach that ran along the waterfront to my left and right, sandy in most parts and stony in others. The town was built on a flat of land that rose about fifteen feet above the beach, meaning that the sand ended in an abrupt stone wall.

A steep set of stone stairs brought me up to the street level, where I was surprised to find a long road lined with four-story buildings on both sides that looked like they dated back to the nineteenth century.

"Whoa," I said, stepping onto the road properly for the first time. As I came around the corner it was like stepping onto the set of some picturesque postcard town. Cars came and went down the street, the sidewalks were busy with the footfall of people going about their daily business. I stared up at the well-preserved architecture surrounding me, finding myself oddly inspired by the heritage of this town.

I don't know what I had expected from the town of Compass Cove, but so far I was impressed.

"Morning!" a rotund and cheery-looking woman sang to me as she walked past. I smiled at her, but I was so taken aback by the pleasant greeting I kind of just stared at her awkwardly as she carried on down the street. Back in the city the atmosphere had been a little bit different; I spent most of my time avoiding the eyes of people I saw in the street. The last time I made the mistake of catching someone's eye it was some drugged out guy that threatened to shank me if I 'took his leprechaun.'

I was glad to be far away.

"Beauty isn't she?" a gravelly and familiar voice said in my ear as I found myself staring up at the buildings. I jumped and saw Gordo standing behind me. I hadn't realized he'd walked this way with me.

"You almost gave me a heart attack!" I remarked.

"My hairdresser had a heart attack once when he was cutting my hair. Here's the kicker though, he *finished the haircut*. It was a sunny day in July and—"

"I'm going to stop you right there; I'm not falling for another one of your shaggy dog stories. This town is amazing, how old are these buildings?"

"You're no fun," he said at my dismissal of another yarn. "Three-quarters of the town dates back to pre-1900. Back then it was mostly a fishing town, but work dried up for ten years when all the fish left."

I blinked very slowly, almost having to admire Gordo's gift for making things up at any opportune moment. "Sure, sure they did. Anyway, I'm looking for 35 Eureka Street. Do you know where it is?"

"Down that way," he said, pointing to the right. "Three blocks down and take a left, past the bronze statue of the candlemaker fighting a bear."

Once again, I found myself staring at him, wondering why I even bothered. "I thought you had a moose head to pick up?"

"Oh, I do. You looked a little lost though, so I thought I'd stop and see if you needed help. Bye now!" With that, Gordo skipped off down the sidewalk, heading in the opposite direction to this supposed address. It seemed that Gordo was incapable of opening his mouth without telling a lie—I didn't get the impression this was a malicious habit, perhaps he was just an unusual man that struggled to separate fantasy from reality.

Doubting his instructions, I headed off in the direction he pointed. I suspected I'd probably be better heading in the opposite direction myself, but it looked like there was an information center at the end of the block, so I could just stop in there and ask for help.

Two minutes later I stepped through the door of that information center, a sleepy little building with walls full of pamphlets advertising local attractions. *Coal World, Jill's Eel Zoo,* and *World's 3rd Biggest Ball of Yarn* were among the stellar offerings. There was a man behind a counter, his shirt sleeves rolled up to his elbows and his glasses down at the end of his nose.

He was sitting upright in a desk chair snoring loudly.

"Ahem?" I said as I approached the counter. The man woke with a start, jumping so much that he fell back out of his chair and scrambled to his feet a second later.

"I wasn't sleeping!" he said.

"Relax, I'm not going to snitch on you," I said with a bemused smile, taking in the man. He was tall, lanky, with short black hair, thick-rimmed glasses and a face that reminded me of a scared marsupial. With a bowtie and suspenders, he looked like he'd be right at home in a barbershop quartet.

"I appreciate it. Sorry, I'm just a little bit tired. My wife had triplets recently. It's been an…" He stared off into the distance while trying to find the word. I could tell from his red eyes and the empty coffee cups on his desk that he was fighting off the effects of sleep deprivation. I stood there for a good thirty seconds before I realized he wasn't going to say anything else.

"Uh, hello?" I said, waving my hand in front of his face.

"An interesting three months!" he said in startlement, snapping out of his stupor. "Sorry, I keep doing that. Falling asleep with my eyes open." He picked up a framed picture from his desk and showed it to me. "That's me and my wife, Brie, and the three girls. Twyla, Lyla, and Kyla."

"Cute names…" I said, handing the picture back to him. "Your wife is very pretty."

"Oh, Brie? She sure is. She was the homecoming queen; I was voted 'most likely to work at the Compass Cove flight center.'"

"Talk about a specific superlative. But hey, guess they were wrong?"

"Oh no, they totally nailed it. I *do* work at the flight center, have done since I finished school. I volunteer here once a month. I'm proud to say I've overlooked seven launches in that time." He quickly added, "At the center, not here. You can't launch a rocket from an information center!"

"Ah, *that* kind of flight center, got it. I was thinking planes. So, you work with rockets? That's cool!"

"Yes, it's very exciting, we do tours on Tuesdays and Thursdays if you want to visit." He handed me a leaflet from nowhere, on the front of which there was a rocket and the words '*Compass Cove Flight Center – Journey to the Stars!*'. "I'm Howard, by the way," he added.

"Nice to meet you, Howard. I'm Zora."

"It's a pleasure, so what can I help you with? I've not seen your face around here before so you must be a tourist!" he said with a smile.

"I'm looking for 35 Eureka Street, could you direct me to it?"

"Ah yes, that's an easy one!" he said, hopping out of his chair and walking up to the glass window that ran along the front of the information shop. "Head out of the shop, take a right and carry on down three blocks. Once you get to the bronze statue of the candlemaker fighting the bear take a left and you're on Eureka." My mouth dropped open as Howard basically repeated Gordo's directions word-for-word. "Is something the matter?" he asked.

I laughed to myself. "It's nothing. I already received directions from someone, and they were the exact same. I thought they were lying though. I guess I should be a little more trusting."

"With the roads washed out you must have taken the boat to get here, which means you've had the pleasure of meeting old Gordo. I take it he was your source. It's heads or tails whether he tells you the truth or not, that's kind of his thing," Howard said and chuckled.

"You know him?" I asked.

"Oh, everyone knows everyone around here," Howard said. "If you're here much longer than a week you'll find that out. How long are you in town for anyway?"

"I'm not sure at the moment. I kind of came here on a whim after a mysterious visit from a long-lost relative. I guess it all depends on what I find at this address."

"Sounds mysterious!" Howard said with his toothy smile. "Well, if there's anything else I can do for you, be sure to come back to the information point. I won't be here until next month of course… but there's always someone here to help out!"

I thanked Howard and left, heading back down the street, the same direction that Gordo had initially pointed.

While walking I took in the town and its pleasant atmosphere, regarding the many different shops lining Main Street and the colorful array of people walking in and out of them. It looked like there were lots of little individual businesses here, and I didn't see signs for any big franchise businesses that have taken over every little town these days.

Even the bank was unknown to me. Like the rest of the shops, it was located in one of the stunning four-story heritage buildings that lined the street. The sign over the door said, *'Moon Bear Bank'*, a surprisingly cute name for a business like a bank.

I carried on down the street until, sure enough, I came to a big bronze statue depicting a man with candles fighting back a huge grizzly bear. As I wasn't operating on any particular schedule, I figured it wouldn't hurt to take a closer look at the sign on the base of the statue. I just *had* to know what this was supposed to represent. The sign said:

October 13th, 1841. On this day the honorable Abraham Wick fought off and defeated the Great Bear, claiming the cove and the surrounding areas for his party of settlers. A trained candlemaker, Abraham is shown here fighting off the Great Bear with candles. Historical records tell us he actually used an elephant rifle.

I stepped back from the sign and blinked a few times, pondering the absolute insanity of that brief text. If I didn't know any better, I would have guessed Gordo was responsible for the story somehow; it just seemed too unplausible to be true.

"Is everyone in this town insane?" I muttered to myself, shaking my head and heading off in the direction of the address I was looking for. A few moments later I found myself standing outside 35 Eureka Street. For some reason I had it in my mind this would be a residential address, but I was looking at a closed bakery, its windows and doors painted with flaking blue, white, and pink paint. The sign over the door said, *'Sugar Rush'.* I approached the boarded-up door, peered through the windows at the dark interior, and noticed dust on the floor.

It looked like this place had been shut for some time.

"Hello?" I said, knocking on the door. There wasn't a buzzer or doorbell in sight, and judging from the interior I wasn't going to get an answer anytime soon. Still, this was the address I'd been given. I let out a sigh, turned away from the door, and sat down on the stone step in its porch.

Was this all just some big ruse? I'd taken it in good faith the mysterious woman claiming to be my aunt had a reason to travel halfway across the country, but for all I know I could have dreamt up the entire thing. Still, I *did* have the map and note she gave me, and the memory of her being in my apartment didn't feel like a dream.

Andino. I bet that good for nothing landlord came up with all this just to get me out of the apartment. It was more high effort than I'd expect from him, but I wouldn't put it past him. He'd picked the furthest possible town and sent me on a wild goose chase. *And I bought it, like a sucker!*

Just then a little black cat came down the sidewalk and nudged my hand with its head, offering a little *meow* as it did so.

"What's that, you want to know what's wrong, kitty?" I asked, imagining the cat was asking me. "Oh nothing, you're just looking at the world's biggest sucker. I came halfway across the country on a wild goose chase, and there's no goose at the end." I let out another sigh. "Still, it looks like there are lot of individual businesses here. Maybe I could get a job, the local economy looks strong, so I'm choosing to see that as the silver lining."

"*Meow,*" the cat said again. It turned away and walked back in the direction it came, stopping at a side alley on the shop corner. It sat down, looked at me, and then sort of jerked its head in the direction of the alleyway.

"Did... did you just motion for me to follow you?" I asked in doubt.

Things got stranger then. The cat looked like it nodded, and it jerked its head at the alley again. *"Meow, meow!"* it said.

"Well, I've officially lost my mind. Homeless, jobless, *and* insane. I've got the full sweep now." Of course, there was drugs too, but I had no interest in that sort of thing, or the money for it. "What the heck, let's follow a cat." I pushed myself up and followed the cat to the alley entrance. Once there the cat took off up the alleyway, turned around another corner at the end and disappeared out of sight.

It occurred to me then that this might be some sophisticated mugging effort dreamed up by some criminals with too much time and a talent for training cats. If that was the case, then they really ought to rethink their direction in life. Imagine being able to make a cat do anything and waste that talent on petty theft? Just the thought made me angry!

I walked into the alley and around the corner, where I saw the cat and the back of the bakery. "This better not be a mugging," I said to the little cat. "I'm just saying, if I was your trainer, we'd have a show in Vegas together or something. You are squandering your potential!"

The cat simply responded with, *'Meow'*, but I took its response to mean, *"What the hell are you talking about, lady?!"*

"Listen, I don't know; I've obviously lost my mind. Why am I back here, what could you have possibly—" Just then I realized two things. The back door of the bakery was open a crack, and inside I could hear someone calling out for help.

"Help!" came the desperate cry. "Help me, help me, someone help me! He's going to kill me!"

"So, this is a Lassie moment," I said to the cat, adrenaline beating through me as I stared at the open door. "I guess I better get in there!" I stared at the door and took a moment to find the courage before I ran inside.

Here goes nothing!

CHAPTER 4

I burst through the door expecting to find myself in the thick of it, but the bakery back door opened into a corridor first of all. To my left a set of stairs climbed to the floor above, and on my right, there was another door slightly ajar. It was through this door I could see a kitchen, and I could hear the cries for help.

In the corner I saw an old tire iron, so I picked it up, burst through the door, and held my impromptu weapon above my head. From the cries I was expecting to see a man attacking a woman, so when I saw a lone girl by herself reading lines from a paper you can imagine my confusion.

Immediately I realized I had made a drastic mistake, but the poor girl reading lines on her own in the kitchen must have seen things quite differently. There she was minding her own business when a stark raving lunatic burst through the door holding a tire iron as a weapon.

She took one look at me and screamed, and in the heat of the moment I found myself screaming too. For a few seconds that was all we seemed to do, both lost in this tragic spiral of useless adrenaline and panic.

Things really took a turn then when she pulled some sort of stick out of her pocket and pointed it at me, still screaming as she did so. I have no idea what happened then, but a surge of wind lifted me up off the floor and slammed me into the ceiling, pinning me against it while weird bindings of light wrapped around my wrists and ankles, effectively keeping me suspended there.

Now my screaming really jumped up to the next level. Somehow, I was tied against the ceiling, looking down at this strange girl, who was still pointing a stick at me and screaming. The buck for confusion had now passed over to me, and in a second of more blind panic I decided that dropping my weapon would be a good idea. I figured it would show her I'm not a threat, demonstrate that this is all just a misunderstanding. One very loud, confusing, misunderstanding.

I dropped the tire iron and of course it hit the poor girl right in the face. She let out a yelp like a small dog getting stepped on, threw her stick and papers everywhere, and brought both her hands to her face before dropping to the ground and writhing around in pain.

Whatever she did to pin me to the ceiling came undone at that same moment, the bindings of light breaking into nothingness, causing me to plummet back to the ground and land on the girl I'd just dropped a tire iron on.

She must have thought I was attacking her again because she shrieked and flung her legs around in blind panic as she tried to get away, accidentally catching me straight in the eye with one of her heavy black boots. The wayward kick sent me spinning. I bashed my head on the kitchen table and dropped to the ground again.

All in all, it had to be twenty seconds of absolute chaos and lunacy, the two of us both screaming and wailing in confusion during that entire time. Now we were both on the ground, writhing and groaning as we whimpered over our collective wounds.

"I'm sorry, I'm sorry, I'm sorry!" I said over and over again, clutching my rapidly swelling eye as I sat up, my other hand hovering in front of me to signal surrender.

The girl sitting on the floor across from me was pinching her nose, two bright torrents of red running down the center of face. "What in the… what the heck was that?!" she said. Her voice was a little nasally because she was pinching her nose, but in a normal situation I got the impression it was high-pitched and timid.

"I think this is all one big understanding," I said, slowly moving to my knees to get up from off the floor. I didn't realize I was still under the kitchen table, and I smashed my head again, dropping back to the floor for a third time. "I thought you were being attacked."

"I was! By you!" the girl cried.

"Well, that was an accident too. I didn't mean to drop a tire iron on your face. I was freaking out after you stuck me on the ceiling with… with whatever that was!" I said, pointing at the weird stick that seemed to defy the laws of the universe. In a saner moment I probably could have made the magic connection, but adrenaline is very gifted at turning normal people into idiots.

"Forgive me, but it's a little alarming to be minding your own business, only for someone to burst in a moment later holding a weapon!" she shouted.

"I thought you were being attacked! You were shouting for help!"

"I was rehearsing lines for a play!" the girl exclaimed, pointing at the scattered sheets lying across the floor.

"I realize that *now*," I said, my tone suggesting she was pointing out the obvious. "I had a Lassie moment with this cat outside and at first I wasn't sure if I should follow him because I considered that maybe a smart thief had trained this cat to lure girls down the—"

"The kitchens on fire," the girl interrupted. She jumped to her feet, and I did so too, catching my shoulder on the underside of the table just for good measure. As I stood up, I saw a few of her sheets had landed on a candle and were now up in flame. That flame had spread to a stack of kitchen towels and—well yes, the kitchen was on fire.

"What do we do?!" I shouted.

"Wand, wand, wand!" the girl said, spinning around and looking for her wand. I realized what she was talking about when I saw the stick on the floor she had dropped earlier; it had rolled under the kitchen table. The rational part of my brain said this was crazy, but I jumped to the floor, grabbed the wand, and whacked my head on the table again as I jumped up.

"Here!" I said, thrusting the wand in her direction. It was only then that I realized the wand was broken in two.

"It's… it's broken!" she said in absolute dismay as she took the wand. "I can't do anything with this!" Both of us looked at the fire, which was starting to get worryingly out of hand.

"Uh…" I drawled helpfully, my panicking eyes setting up on a fire extinguisher. "There!" I said, running over to the fire extinguisher and grabbing it. I ripped the red tag from the nozzle, pointed it at the fire, and squeezed the trigger. Just as I did my bloody-nosed acquaintance shouted, *'Wait!'* but it was too late.

I had the extinguisher the wrong way, and the pair of us were blasted in the face with a stinging cloud of white smoke that fountained out everywhere until the room was a void of disorientating snowy fog. I let go of the handle, but it must have stuck because it just kept firing everywhere until the extinguisher was empty.

"Shut it off, shut it off!" the girl screamed.

"I can't; it's malfunctioning!"

As such, the following minute was another spectacular display of confused screaming and running around as we tried to vacate the room. I heard a loud clatter of pans, I ran into a countertop, and when I tried to head towards the door the girl and I collided headfirst and hit the ground, writhing and groaning again in our mutual clumsiness.

When the clouds from the fire extinguisher finally cleared, I sat up and blinked very slowly, holding the various parts of my body that hurt. The girl sat up across from me, looking just as worse for wear.

"Hey, look on the bright side," I said weakly. "The fire's out."

The girl now looked a real mess, her hair everywhere, and she was covered in white from head to toe, her mouth and chin caked in dry blood. There was a thousand-yard-stare in her eyes, and I think for a second neither of us wanted to move again in case we somehow caused ourselves any further injury. "Who are you?" she asked in a defeated way.

"I'm Zora," I said. "I was told to come here. Maybe we should start again?"

"No. Let's not repeat *any* of that," the girl said quickly and pushed herself up to her feet. She came over and helped me up too. Looking around, I saw the kitchen was in a real bad state. "There's only one thing that can solve this," she said.

"Magic?" I asked, curious to see more.

"No, a cup of tea and some cookies. Follow me and try not to cause any more trouble."

"I'll try, but I'm making no promises," I said as I followed her out of the room.

* * *

WE STEPPED into the corridor that I'd initially entered from and headed up the set of steep stairs. There was another door right at the top, and as we stepped through that I found myself in a cute apartment with high ceilings. The space felt open and airy, well-lit by large windows that overlooked the street at the front of the building.

In a way it reminded me of my studio apartment back in the city, half of the space acted as a lounge area, while the other half was a kitchen and diner. Unlike my old apartment there was actually plenty of space to pull this off.

The door entered into the kitchen and dining area of the apartment at first. Vintage mint green cabinets and charcoal black countertops made up the kitchen, along with a checkered black and white floor. It looked as though the kitchen was fairly new but designed carefully in a way that it appeared older. I walked just beyond the kitchen; there was a table and chairs, and then the lounge half of the apartment began.

Hardwood floors ran throughout the rest of the apartment, and in the lounge a huge plush rug adorned with moons sat underneath an old Asian coffee table and two large couches that faced each other on either side of the table.

On the wall to my left there was a huge bookshelf stacked to the brim, and on the exposed brick wall next to that there hung a large tapestry, a midnight blue sky embellished with a silver moon and stars.

On my right there was an open stone fireplace and an old box TV sitting on a large wooden cabinet. I walked up to the large windows that looked out on the street below, finding myself hypnotized as I stared at cars and people passing by. A cushioned windowsill ran directly along the windows, and I imagined it would make a great reading spot.

The view also overlooked part of a park, giving a city view with trees and nature. I turned back around to face my mysterious companion. "Your apartment is beautiful," I gasped.

"Thanks, but it's not mine. I just come here sometimes to get some peace and quiet. I'm the only one that can come in for some reason—the kitchen and upstairs anyway. I clean what I can."

"What do you mean you're the only one that can come in?" I asked.

"Ever since Constance died—she was my aunt—it's like she's trying to keep people out of the old bakery. No one's been in there since she died. I'm Zelda by the way."

"Zora," I said again. "Sorry for the calamity downstairs. I really did think you were in trouble."

"Just reading lines!" she said with a nervous smile. I don't know whether it was our unfortunate meeting that had left her rattled, but she was a bundle of nervous energy, quiet, timid, and not one for eye contact. "I'll, uh, get towels, one sec."

Zelda disappeared through another door branching off from the apartment. It looked like there was more to explore beyond this initial impressive offering. I wanted to sit on the cushioned windowsill and stare out at the town, but I caught sight of myself in a tall mirror on the wall behind me and saw a mess.

Head to toe I was covered in white from the fire extinguisher, and my hair was all over the place. I looked like a scarecrow's ghost. I got closer to the mirror to inspect my injuries and saw the beginnings of a black eye where Zora had accidentally caught me with her boot.

Talk about an interesting first day in town.

A *'Meow!'* pulled my attention from the mirror, and I saw the little black cat from outside sitting on the cushioned windowsill. My disastrous encounter with Zelda was obviously not the cat's fault, but I couldn't help feeling that he was partly responsible.

"Are you supposed to be in here?" I said reproachfully. "Don't you think you've already caused enough mischief?"

The cat blinked back at me with its large green eyes. Zelda came back into the room holding two large towels. "Don't bother with him," she said and handed me one of the towels. "Hermes hasn't uttered a word since Constance died over a year ago."

I stared at Zelda for a second, wondering what she had meant by that. "Yes... well, he was pretty adamant at getting me inside the bakery. This is the cat that shepherded me in here."

"Familiar," she said.

"What?" I asked.

"He's not a cat, he's a—" Zelda paused and gave me a funny look. "Wait, don't you know that? You are a—well you'd have to be to get in the kitchen, but then you're also acting quite—" She kept tripping over herself with confusing half-sentences until I interrupted.

"Am I missing something?"

"No. No!" she said quickly. "Uh listen, there's a bathroom through there. Wash yourself up and I'll put the kettle on. Do you like cake?"

"Does a one-legged duck swim in a circle?" I asked.

"What?" Zelda repeated in confusion.

"It's an expression. *Yes*, a one-legged duck does swim in circles. And *yes*, I do like cake."

"Why does the duck only have one leg, did someone hurt it?"

"It's just an expression, the duck isn't real."

"I've seen two-legged ducks swim in circles though. Ducks can be quite graceful; a lot of people give them a hard time."

"Do they?" I asked in incredulity. "You know what, scratch that. I'd love some cake. I'll just go and wash up." Zelda nodded with another unsure smile, and I headed into the bathroom. I washed up as best as I could, trying to dust the white powder off my clothes. I managed to get most of it off my face and hands and dragged a comb through my hair to make myself look a little less like the girl that crawls out of the TV in that horror film.

I came back into the main room of the apartment and saw that Zelda had already placed a tray of cakes and a teapot with two cups on the coffee table in the lounge. I joined her at the table, sinking into the comfortable couch opposite to her.

I had some tea, a bit of cake, and immediately felt a little better. A warm rush of comfort swept through me. "This cake is amazing," I said. "I feel revitalized!"

"Hmm..." Zelda said cryptically across the table, looking at me in an examining way. She swallowed some cake and had a sip of her tea too. "So, what are you doing here? I mean, you're not from around town, are you?"

"No, actually someone brought me here. I probably should have opened with that." I put down my cup and pulled the note from out of my bag, passing it over to Zelda. She read it and a look of alarm and confusion came over her.

"This is from Liza!" she remarked. "How do you know Liza?"

"I don't. She just appeared in my apartment randomly a few nights ago and did all these weird magic tricks. She said I have family here, she also said I'm a witch. I don't know if she's one of these pagan types, maybe she meant Wiccan or something like that? But then again she did turn a fire poker into a silk scarf—"

"Liza visited you?" Zelda asked. "How very odd. So, she already told you you're a witch?"

"She did. To be honest I thought she was nuts, but then I did just see you tie me to a ceiling with magical light…"

"Ah, so you're only just learning about magic. That explains it then."

"Explains what?"

"You have to be a witch to get in the kitchen of this bakery. Constance set up that charm many years ago. So, the fact that you're in here pretty much confirms you *are* a witch, but you look so starry-eyed by magic I can tell you're new, and you also don't know what a familiar is."

I had to think for a moment as I took this information in. My gut reaction was to assume this girl—and the mysterious Liza—were both crazy, but I *had* seen empirical evidence of magic existing multiple times now. I mean, Zelda put me on a ceiling, it doesn't get much more in your face than that.

"Can you do more?" I asked. "I want to see what's possible."

"Without my wand? No, not really. I'll have to get a new one from Sabrina, she's my cousin; she runs a magic shop in town."

"So, you need a wand to do magic?"

"No, but I'm lazy and overly reliant on it. I guess I could try and do something small…" Zelda pointed her hand at the table and snapped her fingers. A bowl of sugar cubes appeared, spinning slightly and rattling until it came to a stop.

"Whoa!" I said, positively jumping out of my chair. "That was amazing!"

Zelda laughed nervously. "It's just a bowl of sugar cubes!"

"But, but that's amazing!" I said again. "Where did they come from?"

"The kitchen," she said, looking very confused. "Oh, the cakes as well."

"The cakes?"

"I'm a kitchen witch mostly, so most of my power goes into making food. I have a café in town with my other cousin, Celeste. You mentioned you felt revitalized; that was because of the magic in the cake. It's meant to lift you up." Zelda popped another bit of cake in her mouth and smiled. "So, how are you related to the family? Liza hasn't mentioned anything about you."

"I don't know. She appeared in my apartment, and she disappeared just as quickly. I kind of expected to see her here to be honest."

Zelda laughed, as if the idea was hysterical. "Who, Liza? No. She's a very busy woman and she doesn't have a lot of time. She doesn't come around here much."

"Who is she to you?"

"My grandmother. Quite a lot of people are afraid of her, but she is nice. She just has high expectations of people."

"She said she was my grandmother too!" I said. "That means we must be cousins!"

"Peculiar!" Zelda said, her face looking more bemused now. "Who is your mother?"

"I don't know," I admitted. "My dad raised me, and he and my mother parted when I was very young."

"Sounds a little like my mother," Zelda replied. "She disappeared when I was two. How old are you? I'm twenty-three."

"Twenty-five. Hey, I always wanted a younger cousin! It was just me and my dad growing up. Do you know my dad? Nolan Yates?"

Zelda shook her head. "Never heard of him. Maybe your mom was one of Liza's sister's daughters. What would that be relation wise?"

"A sibling of a grandparent is a grandaunt, that means my mom was your first cousin once removed, and I must be your second cousin," I explained.

Zelda blinked at me in a very vacant way. "How did you figure that out so easily?!"

"I took a filler credit in community college on genealogy; it's actually quite interesting once you get the hang of it."

"I'll take your word for it!" Zelda laughed. "Well, sorry for the lukewarm reception. Liza isn't around much. I can try and call her, but she's quite hard to get hold of."

"Sure, that's fine by me." I said. Zelda got up and walked over to a flamingo housephone on a side table. Up until now I'd somehow failed to notice the amusingly garish phone. Zelda dialed a number and tapped her foot while waiting. "Liza, it's me, Zelda. There's a girl called Zora at Aunt Constance's place. She said you told her to come here. Call me back when you get a chance." Zelda put the phone down and sat back down on the couch. "Well, I tried. She's probably going to be at work for several more hours. Where are you staying?"

"I haven't got a place sorted yet," I said. "I kind of rolled into town on fumes."

"You can stay here for a night if you like, if you can put up with Constance messing you around."

"Constance?"

"My aunt, this is her place, and the bakery below is hers too. She died just over a year ago. I've never seen her ghost, but she likes to cause trouble."

"Ghosts are real?" I balked.

"Yes, but they don't show their faces very often. Apparently, some witches can see them, but it's not common. Anyway, like I said, I'm really the only one that comes here. You're welcome to stay until you find your feet. I'll double-check with Celeste and Sabrina—they're Constance's daughters—but I can't imagine they'll have a problem with it."

"Are you sure I'm okay to stay here? Aren't you practicing your lines?"

"My lines? Oh," Zelda laughed and rolled her eyes. "I mean that was just a silly little thing. I've not got a part or anything."

"There must be an audition, right? That's why you were practicing. What's it for?"

"Uh… there's a play down at the local theatre, they do a new production every three months. I picked up a copy just to see the script, I'm not actually going to audition."

"What? Why?! You were great! You convinced me you were being attacked!"

Zelda laughed nervously. "I'm not an actress," she said dismissively. "I could never actually get a part in a play."

"I wouldn't doubt yourself so much. If you pluck up the courage to audition, I think you'd definitely get the part."

"That's very nice of you," Zelda said, her cheeks filling with red. "But it was just a silly little game; I'm not actually interested. Anyway, I think I should—oh!" she said, sitting to attention and then standing just as quickly. "Nana! I thought you were at the hospital!"

Turning around, I saw Liza in the kitchen behind us. She was wearing the same thick white coat I had seen her in back at my apartment, her black shades obscuring her eyes, her short silver hair like a crown of ice.

"What did I tell you about calling me nana?" she said offhandedly. "It ages me, Zelda, it ages me, darling!"

"Sorry, I'm just surprised to see you. You're usually working," Zelda said timidly. Liza and Zelda were opposites as far as personality was concerned. Zelda was a shrinking violet, Liza? Some sort of man-eating plant from the Amazon.

"I was," Liza said coldly. "I popped over after I got your message." Something told me there was literal magic behind the word *popped*. Liza walked forward slowly, her heels echoing around the room. She looked at me and smiled. "So, you made it."

"I did, but I must admit I'm very confused. You disappeared so quickly."

"I have places to be, Zora darling, I can't waste all my time dillydallying." Liza looked Zelda and I both over, her brow furrowing in disapproval. "What happened to you both? It looks like a pack of gibbons got to you."

"There was a little confusion when I first arrived, but it's cleared up now," I said.

Liza noted the tea and cakes on the table. "So, you're already acquainted? That's good. Saves me a job."

"Would you like a drink, Liza?" Zelda said quickly. "Cake?"

"Relax, Zel, I haven't time, but thank you. I just wanted to see that Zora here was settling in."

"I am, I still have lots of questions though. Like why you brought me here, and how we're related." I looked at Zelda. "We're like second cousins or something, right?"

Once again Liza looked baffled. "Oh goodness, you really are a pair of simpletons. You haven't figured it out yet?"

"Figured what out?" I asked.

"You're sisters," she said as if it was the most mundane thing in the world. "Can't you tell?!"

CHAPTER 5

Liza's reveal took the wind out of my sails, and looking at Zelda she was just as shocked. I felt the weight go from my legs and I sank to the couch in shock. Zelda did the exact same thing, almost at the same time.

"Good grief!" Liza said, strutting over to the table and snatching a cookie from the plate. "You really mean to say you didn't figure it out?! Witches are meant to have an innate sense for this sort of thing!" Liza took a bite out of her gingersnap, strutting around the apartment back and forth as she spoke. "I mean really, it should come as no shock. Look at the two of you, you're a mirror image of one another!"

I really hadn't considered it until now, but now Liza had brought it to my attention there was no denying an uncanny similarity between myself and Zelda. We both had long dark hair that went past our shoulders, straight and flat— (I constantly tried to give my hair some kind of volume, but it never obeyed). I had bangs and Zelda's hair was parted down the middle, but our faces were very alike: strong brows, sharp cheekbones, and squarish jaws with a pointed chin.

I'd never really thought of myself as pretty, but Zelda definitely was. There was probably some sort of cognizant dissonance going on there because we really were clones of one another. I was two years older apparently, but there wasn't enough between us to tell the difference.

"A sister!" Zelda whispered in shock. Her face was entirely white now, and she looked like she was going to pass out. She looked at Liza. "Why did you never tell me?!"

"Don't put this on me!" Liza said defensively. "I never knew! Blame that blasted daughter of mine, Tabatha, running around and having children in secret!"

"Wait a second," I said. "You know something about my mother?" I paused and looked at Zelda. "I mean, *our* mother?"

"Let's not start with that right now," Liza said, dramatically holding one hand to her head while she held the other hand in the air like a diva shooing away the press. "Tabatha was an enigma to me as much as she was to anyone else. I only found out you existed last week for goodness' sake."

"Who was she?" I asked. "Why didn't I grow up with a mother?" Again, I looked at Zelda. She said her mother disappeared when she was two. "Neither of us did!" Zelda stared at Liza in expectation, just the same as me. I think we both got the impression she knew something we didn't, whether that was accurate or not.

"Let's get something clear right away. Tabatha didn't share secrets with anyone, least of all me! She had her own thing going on, and she was very much wrapped in it. I don't know why she kept you a secret," she said to me, "and I don't know where she disappeared to all those years ago!" she said to Zelda.

A moment of tension beat through the room. Liza strutted back over to the table and snatched another three cookies, shoving them into her mouth quickly. "Good batch, Zel, really they are."

"Thanks, Na—I mean, *Liza*."

"So, you really don't know anything about our mother?" I said to the woman that was supposedly my grandmother.

"Not a jot, darling. Now your Aunt Constance on the other hand. She was a dear. Never gave her mother any trouble. She's the reason you're here, Zora. Constance came to visit me two weeks ago; her ghost appeared to me on the anniversary of her death."

"You never told me that!" Zelda said in startlement.

"Hush now, Zelda," Liza said, not taking her eyes off me.

"Why would Aunt Constance want me here?" I asked. "I never heard of her until twenty minutes ago!"

"No, but she was secretly in touch with your father. She kept in touch with him all these years. Constance's ghost led me to a hidden box of mail. That's how I ended up tracking you down, Zora."

"But why does she want me here?"

"I guess that remains to be seen," Liza said. "But let's get one thing straight, you're a Wick and you belong here in your hometown. This town is your heritage! These are your people! This is your—" A beeper started bleeping on Liza's hip; she peered at the screen and rolled her eyes. "Blast and drat, I've got to go, something's come up. I'll catch up with you both later. Show her around town, Zel, and don't take her to your lot!"

Before I could even question what that meant Liza vanished in a blink of shimmering silver smoke. One second she was there, the next she was gone.

"What does she mean by 'your lot?'" I asked Zelda.

"Umm... so there's this whole family dynamic. I guess I'm kind of the black sheep of the family?"

"What, why?"

"So, two of the oldest magical families in the town are the Wicks and the Brewers. Both come from very different cuts of cloth, but good wizards and witches in their own right. Wicks come from money and tend to have good jobs and good insight."

"And the Brewers?" I asked.

"Uh, criminal records, trailer parks, moonshine, trouble—you get the idea. My mother was a Wick, and my Daddy is a Brewer, Billy Brewer to be precise."

"These Brewers are bad?"

"Not bad necessarily, but I guess they can be hot-blooded. We've made some mistakes."

"So, you're some sort of hybrid between the two families," I remarked with amusement. "I guess Liza doesn't like that side of the family." Liza was a fur and pearls type. To think that one of her granddaughters was the spawn of a trailer park probably drove her up the wall.

"Neither side likes the other, it's always been that way. They are strong in different ways though. The Brewers have a good grasp on wild magic, the Wicks are more book-learned."

I leaned back into the couch, coming back to the fact once again that I was staring at my little sister. "So, we're half-sisters. Same mother, different fathers. That's pretty wild. I always wanted a little sister."

"I always wanted a pet racoon, but I guess having an older sister is cool too," Zelda said and smiled. I found myself joining in. "Celeste and Sabrina were sort of like my sisters growing up. I spent quite a lot of time here with them. Constance was practically a mother to me."

"So, there's Liza, and she has two daughters, Constance and Tabatha?"

"Yup. Tabatha—our mother—disappeared when I was two, and Constance died last year."

"So, both Liza's children are gone."

Zelda nodded sadly. "Yeah, Liza means well, but I don't think people are her strong point. She's always been a little distant and cold, but it got worse after Aunt Constance died."

"And Constance has two daughters, Celeste and Sabrina?"

"Yup! There's only a year between them. Sabrina's a year younger than me, and Celeste a year younger than her. They're both like super driven and successful; it's kind of annoying actually. Like I said, I'm the black sheep of the family."

"I thought you said you worked at this café with Celeste?"

"Well yeah, I do, but it's her café. She gave me the job, most likely out of pity." I was quickly getting a read on Zelda, and she struck me as one of those types that constantly downplayed her own achievements and belittled her potential. She was obviously capable of more than she realized. "Say, where are your things?" she asked.

"I left my car back at a gas station in Sacketsville. All my stuff is in there. Actually, it's not even my car, it's a rental. This girl at the station told me my things would be safe there."

"Tall, skinny, brown hair pulled back in a ponytail?"

"Yes! I think she said her name was Ellie."

"I know her, Ellie's a good egg. I think your things will be safe. I take it you probably know about the roads being washed out then, which means you most likely met Gordo—"

"Yes, I had the pleasure of meeting Gordo. He is… *quite* the storyteller."

Zelda laughed. "Hey, you cottoned on faster than most. Listen there's a car ferry twice a day with the roads being out. If we hurry down to the water, we can get your car and your stuff over here, and I can help you unpack."

"You're sure?" I asked. "You don't have other things to do?"

"It's my day off from the café. I'll be straight up with you. I don't have many friends or hobbies. Things can be pretty dull around here. I usually hang out with Celeste and Sabrina, but they're both working right now."

"Alright then; I guess we'll go and get my things. You can point out all the interesting landmarks on the way!"

"Shouldn't take long," Zelda said with a chuckle, "but sure."

The two of us got our things together and made our way out of the shop via the backdoor, Zelda locking the door as she did so. "By the way," I asked as we made our way back to the street. "The bronze statue of the candlemaker wrestling a bear…"

"Yeah, I know what you're thinking, and it's genuine. Want to know something even crazier? We're supposed to be descended from that dude. If you thought crazy was a new thing in our family then think again, it goes back *many* generations!"

CHAPTER 6

Zelda and I walked back through town along Main Street, Zelda pointing out areas of interest as we walked. It seemed she had a story about every shop and person working there.

"Ooh, we should totally stop at Celeste's café, it's on the way! You can meet her!"

"Okay," I said, feeling excited to meet another long-lost relative. "I started today with literally no family, now I've got a sister and a grandmother. Let's rack up the cousins too. Didn't you say your other cousin has a magic shop?"

"Sabrina? Yes, she does, but her shop is in the other direction. I'd swing by but she's doing an inventory day or something and she always gets super grumpy around inventory day."

"Inventory day?"

"She like counts all the stock in the shop or something. To be honest I'm not totally sure. I always stay out of the way at this time of year. The café's just here, come on!"

Zelda opened the door of *White Rabbit Café*, a cute little pastel colored shop with three stories of vintage architecture stretching above it. I'd actually seen the café on my way to the old bakery; it definitely stood out.

Inside, the café was bright and chic, the décor a combination of pastel pink and crisp white. There were plenty of customers dining in, and behind the counter I saw a short round girl with black lipstick and a nose ring. There was a short queue at the counter, but she waved at Zelda in acknowledgment. Celeste was currently serving an old lady, and behind her a tall guy in sweats was waiting impatiently, tapping his foot and muttering under his breath. I saw Celeste glance at him out the side of her eye more than once.

"And this one?" the old lady asked, pointing at a sandwich in the display.

"That's not gluten free, but I can whip you up one tomorrow if you like. All I have left for gluten free today is—"

"Oh, come on, hurry up!" the tall guy in sweats shouted. The old woman glanced back at him in confusion. Celeste crossed her arms and raised an incredulous brow. "Excuse me?" she said. "Who do you think you're talking to?"

"Just pick a damn sandwich and get out the way, old lady, before we all end up dying in here! We all got places to be!"

"I'll step aside and let this young man order," the old lady offered to Celeste.

"No, that's not necessary. He's leaving," Celeste said, looking at the rude man sternly.

Suddenly the jerk wad stepped up to the counter. "Leaving? Since when? How do you plan on making that happen, huh? Are you threatening me? The customer is always right. I want to speak to your manager. *Now.*"

"Uh, you're speaking to her," Celeste said, not backing down at all. "And she just told you to get out, so *go.*"

The tall jerk in sweats didn't say anything for a second; he leaned in closer and in a desperate attempt to validate his fragile ego he knocked the tip jar off the counter. It was a plastic cup so clattered harmlessly across the floor, but the change inside went everywhere.

"You know who you're messing with, darling?"

"I know who you are, and I'm not afraid of you. Go now, before I call the police," Celeste said as a last warning.

The jerk scoffed. "Whatever, the food here sucks anyway. I'm better off going to the dollar store. I'll save money and get more." He turned around and saw Zelda and me standing directly in front of him. He looked at Zelda and puckered his lips. "Hey, beautiful, what's your number?"

Zelda just looked at the ground, and the jerk stepped forward to brush a strand of hair off her face. Without thinking I jumped forward and grabbed his hand. "What's the matter?" I said. "Didn't your mother teach you to keep your hands to yourself?" I pushed his hand away and he smirked.

"Ooh, I like this one. She's got fire!" He stepped forward to intimidate me and something odd happened then. This split-second fantasy flashed through my head of him tripping over and hitting the ground.

The strangest thing is that is exactly what happened next. The jerk slipped on one of the coins he'd just spilled everywhere, his foot shooting forward so he flew back and hit the ground, landing hard on his back. I took Zelda's hand and stepped over him, so we were next to the counter.

He pushed himself up onto all fours, mumbling something under his breath as he limped to the door. "Don't let the door hit you on the way out!" Celeste called. The bell jangled as he left, then he was gone.

With his departure the atmosphere in the shop immediately brightened again, customers jumping out of their seats to help collect the spilled change. Celeste finished helping the old lady pick out lunch and escorted her to a table.

"He was nice," Zelda quipped as we finally approached the counter.

Celeste shook her head. "He's one of the punks that deals drugs down at the park. Thinks he's some hot shot because his sweatpants pockets are stuffed full of ten-dollar notes. What a loser. Anyway!" Celeste slowly brought her hands over her face, her dark expression illuminating. She looked at me and smiled. "You're new. Thanks for sticking up for Zelda, that took guts. I'm Celeste."

"Oh, I'm Zora," I said, introducing myself back. "And it was no problem. I hate bullies. I haven't got time for them."

"You and me both, girl," Celeste looked at Zelda and shook her head. "It's your day off, dude. Can't you stay away?!"

"I wanted to introduce you to Zora here. She's not actually some random nobody, she's my sister, or half-sister at the least."

Celeste's mouth dropped open and she blinked a few times before responding. "Mother of minty mackerel, what?! There's more of us?!" The entire café paused momentarily to regard the shrieking woman. Celeste noticed the attention and apologized. "Sorry, folks; go back to your meals!" She lowered her voice and resumed, her brow knitting with confusion as she looked at me. "That means we're related?"

"Cousins apparently," I affirmed. "According to Liza anyway."

"I have *so many* questions," she began. "Where have you been, where did you come from, who's your favorite Backstreet Boy, when do we all get to hang out—Oh, go grab a table and I'll have Francesca cover me for twenty, we can talk all about—"

"Hold your horses, Celeste," Zelda interrupted. "We're on a time schedule. We need to run over to Sacketsville to go and pick up Zora's things before the ferry leaves," she explained.

"Zelda!" Celeste said, moaning the word as if she were dying of boredom. "You can't just bring a long-lost relative of mine out of nowhere and expect me not to have a thousand questions." Celeste rolled her eyes and looked at me. "Zel's got it in her head that I'm too talkative."

"I never said that," Zelda said. "But you *do* have the gift of the gab. We were just walking by, so I thought I'd introduce Zora *quickly*. Why don't you come over to the bakery later and we can talk there? Zora's staying there until she gets on her feet."

"Ooh boy, you *are* brave," Celeste commented. "Mom's ghost is a real piece of work, but sure, I can come over, I can—ah shoot, I just remembered I'm supposed to be helping Sab with this darn stock take tonight. I already committed myself to it. I'd suggest you come over and 'help', but Sabrina is a bit of shark this time of year. Maybe hold off on meeting her until that's done. But hey, let me get you a treat for the road. Take anything you want; think of it as a welcome, and thanks for helping me with that jerk!"

Zelda and I both picked a couple of sandwiches for the road, said goodbye to Celeste, and carried on down the street to get back to the water. We ate quickly on a bench, watching people pass by on the sidewalks. Zelda pointed out more businesses and points of interest, and at one point I saw a man and a woman walking down the street carrying a taxidermy moose head playing a saxophone.

"No way," I muttered to myself.

"What's wrong?" Zelda asked.

"When I got off the boat Gordo fed me this story about him needing to pick up something from his taxidermist. I thought he was telling a lie, but I'm pretty sure I just saw the object he described being carried down the street. That saxophone playing moose over there."

Zelda just laughed. "Ah yeah, that's the thing about Gordo. His truths are usually more bizarre than his lies; that's what makes it so hard to separate fact from fiction with that guy. He's pretty eclectic. Ooh, look!" Zelda said as we came around the corner. The buildings on our left ended and the jetty and water beyond came into view. "The ferry's here. Let's go!"

For the second time that day I headed across the cove, this time on the slightly larger car ferry that had been temporarily set up to help move commuters around since the road was washed out.

The ferry was certainly not as entertaining as Gordo's water taxi, but it was definitely a little faster. During the ride I watched the water from the upper deck, taking in the breathtaking scenery of the water and its surrounding coast. "Hey, I've got a question for ya," I said to Zelda. "Gordo said the local economy shut down in the early nineteenth century because 'all the fish left'. That's another one of his tall stories, right?"

"Oh no, apparently that *did* happen," Zelda said.

"What? How?!"

"Yeah, apparently there was a fishing drought. That's why we still have our old architecture. All the other towns along the coast had the money to knock down their buildings and carry on updating with the times, but there was a decade or two where Compass Cove was kind of deserted. I'd say it paid off for us in the long run; we're one of the only towns in America now with a wealth of heritage like our architecture."

"But how can all the fish just leave?!"

"Well, the cove connects to the ocean. It looks like one giant lake from here, but if you zoom out..." Zelda said—she pulled out her phone and zoomed out from our current location on the map. Sure enough on the eastern coast there was a gap in the shoreline that connected the 'water' to the Atlantic Ocean beyond.

"Isn't that technically a bay?" I asked. "I mean, *geographically* speaking."

"What's the difference?" Zelda asked.

"Bays are much larger. Coves are smaller inlets of water."

"It's actually a gulf," a woman in a bright pink rain jacket said from behind us.

"Wait, what's a gulf?" Zelda asked.

"A gulf is a large bay. A bay is a large cove," she explained plainly.

"But everyone calls this place Compass Cove?" I asked.

"Well yeah, it just sounds better," the woman and Zelda both said in unison.

"I think I'm more confused than ever," I said.

Zelda shrugged it off. "Eh, don't let the geeks get you down. Everyone calls it Compass Cove; that's all that you need to worry about. The water does connect to the ocean though, so yeah, the fish can leave if they want to. I think it had something to do with algae, or something boring like that."

"Huh, I guess Gordo deserves more credit than I give him."

"Trust me. You're better off doubting everything Gordo says instead of taking it at face value. He lies enough to justify some skepticism."

It took about twenty minutes for the ferry to reach Sacketsville on the south shore, docking a few blocks over from the gas station. Zelda and I made our way over, got my keys from Ellie at the station, and hurried to get the car back to the ferry before it made its return journey.

Not much later I pulled up outside the front of the old bakery and

Zelda helped me carry a few of my things upstairs. I didn't have much in the way of valuables, mostly I'd just brought clothes, some old photographs, a lamp or two, nothing worth any real money. The most valuable were the photographs of my dad. As long as I had them, I didn't mind losing everything else.

Just as we finished carrying the last of our things inside it started raining, and soon that rain turned into a torrential downpour. We both ran inside and climbed the stairs to Constance's apartment, slightly out of breath as we shut the door behind us and set the last of my things down.

"Man, that rain came out of nowhere!" I said as I made my way to the front of the apartment to the tall glass windows that looked over the street. Rain battered the glass and the roads now, and I heard a crack of lightning somewhere in the distance.

"Welcome to Compass Cove." Zelda chuckled and set a box of my things down on the floor before coming over to examine the storm with me. "The weather here flips on a dime. You'll learn to always have a raincoat with you. I've always got one in my bag. All the locals do!"

"Noted." I sat down on the cushioned windowsill and watched the rain come down. "Man, I could sit here for hours. I love watching the rain."

"It's pretty hypnotic, eh?" Zelda agreed. "I was going to suggest we go out for food, but I'm not sure I want to venture out now. According to my phone it's raining for the rest of the night. How about takeout. Do you like Chinese?"

"Does a one-legged duck swim in circles?" I asked, reiterating my joke from earlier.

"Who is mutilating all these ducks?" Zelda responded. She was joking this time, but still kept a concerned tone. "Like, is there some serial duck mutilator on the loose? If so, why is no one doing anything to stop them?"

I shrugged. "Maybe the ducks have it coming. I hear they're aggressive little psychopaths."

"Wait, really?" Zelda asked. "But they're so cute! Okay, so Chinese... what do you normally like to order?"

"I'll have whatever you're having," I said, stretching and letting out a long yawn. The day was really starting to get to me now. "What's the restaurant?"

"Ping's, it's the best place to get Chinese. There's Dragon Palace in Eureka as well, but it's off-limits at the moment with the roads being washed out."

"Eureka?" I asked. "Isn't that the name of the street we're on?"

"Ah, yeah, it is. It's also the name of the town on the east coast of the cove."

"Right, right. I keep forgetting, four towns around the cove, right."

"Yup! That's how it got its name," she said, scrolling through the menu on her phone. "Compass Cove, a town at each of the four points. Sacket in the South, Wildwood in the West, Eureka in the East, and Compass Cove in the North."

"All of the town names begin with the same letter as their position on the cove, apart from Compass Cove," I noted.

"Yeah, I guess our ancestors were stubborn or just plain stupid; you're not the first one to notice that. I'm thinking of getting the crispy duck, it's pretty great from Ping's. Do you want the same?"

"Hang on a second, are you the duck mutilator?" I joked.

Zelda smiled as she noticed her double standard. "Hey, I said ducks are cute; I never said they're not delicious."

"No judgments here, put me down for the duck too. Let's do this."

"Alright, that's all ordered!" she said with a tap of her finger. "It'll be here in thirty minutes. There's enough time to shower if you want."

"Very much so," I said. "I thought I got most of that extinguisher off me, but I smell like a stale cloud of chemicals." I had all day.

We both managed to fit in a quick shower, and I changed into a fresh set of clothes just as the delivery came. Zelda and I ate the Chinese on the couch while watching some old Nic Cage film on TV.

By about ten it was still raining outside, Zelda let out a long yawn and pushed herself up from the couch as the credits started rolling on the movie. "I'm going to head back to my place and get some sleep," she said while stretching. "I'm working at the café tomorrow morning, so I won't be able to hang until the afternoon."

"That's okay; it'll probably do me some good to explore on my own anyway. Plus, Liza gave me the impression she was coming back at some point. Maybe she can finally explain why she brought me here."

"I wouldn't hold your breath, but yeah, let's swap numbers."

Zelda and I swapped numbers and she headed downstairs to leave, handing me the keys for the building before she went. We were standing in the bakery kitchen on the ground floor, which was still a mess from earlier. "I'll clean this up tomorrow," I said.

"Don't worry about it. Constance will probably sort it out. She's a restless ghost," Zelda replied.

"You're serious about this ghost thing; it's not a joke?" I asked.

Zelda shook her head. "Not a joke. No one's ever really seen her, but—" Zelda paused and looked at the door from the kitchen that led into the bakery. "I guess I should show you this before I leave."

"What?" I asked, following her as she made her way over to the door.

"So, I mentioned earlier that Constance doesn't really like anyone being here. She just about tolerates me being in the kitchen and the apartment to keep the place clean, but the bakery itself. Well... let me just show you."

Zelda opened the door to the bakery itself. All the lights were off, and it was dark. She stepped through the door and suddenly a pan flew at her. Zelda ducked out the way, the pan hit the wall with a loud clatter, and Zelda quickly ducked back through the door before shutting it.

"Someone's in there?!" I asked, my heart pounding slightly in my chest.

"No, that's just Constance's ghost being a jerk. Ever since she died it's been like that. Even Celeste and Sabrina get attacked. Heck, she doesn't even let them in the kitchen. That's why no one has taken over the bakery."

"Huh, how strange."

"Yup, well, sleep tight!" Zelda said cheerily and turned to head out the back door when she stopped. "Oh, also, stay away from Constance's old bedroom too. It's a similar affair. She'll throw something at you, and it's usually the heaviest item she can find. She was an epic fantasy fan, so there are some pretty big books in there for her to do damage with."

"She sounds like a real delight."

"As long as you stay out of those two rooms, you'll be fine. See you tomorrow!"

Once Zelda was gone, I closed the door behind me and locked it. I turned the TV off in the lounge and headed back upstairs to the apartment to go to bed.

There was a door on the wall between the lounge and the kitchen, and it branched off into a small corridor, from which there were four doors. On the left there was the bathroom, and on the right, there were doors to two bedrooms. The door at the end of the corridor was a utility closet.

Zelda had explained the main bedroom had been Constance's, and no one had really been in there since she died. Like the bakery, her ghost didn't seem to like the disturbance, but the guestroom was apparently fine, so I decided to play it safe and sleep in there.

As I opened the door to the guest room I saw Hermes, the little black cat, curled up on the bed. He opened one of his emerald green eyes and glared at me for waking him up.

"How did you even get in here?" I asked. "The door was closed!"

Hermes stretched out, hopped off the bed, and skirted out of the room, brushing past my legs as he did so. I plugged my phone in, pulled back the covers, and lay down on the bed, ready for some much-needed sleep.

I was just about to turn off the bedside light when I turned and saw a transparent blue woman standing at the foot of the bed. I screamed; her face lit up in surprise and she screamed too.

"Who are you?!" I shrieked.

"I'm your Aunt Constance!" she shrieked back. It was less terror, and more like she was copying me in a comedic fashion to try and put me at ease. "Welcome to my house!"

CHAPTER 7

"You're a ghost!" I said, for some reason still shrieking. I wasn't exactly horrified; Constance didn't look scary or anything, but seeing a transparent blue woman at the foot of the bed was more than a little alarming.

"I'm a ghost!" she shrieked back, still matching me for her own amusement. Constance threw her arms in the air and waved her hands around, making a silly face as she did so. She chuckled, her smile fading a little as she composed herself. "Ah but seriously, it is *so* good to finally be seen. Man, it has been a long year of pan throwing, I'll tell you that for free!"

I blinked in disbelief while watching Constance's ghostly specter float about the guestroom, not really sure what to say. "I can see ghosts," I said, mostly for my own benefit.

"Yes, apparently you can. That's why I brought you here. I always knew you'd be the one to get me out of this mess, and I had to wait a whole darned year before I could tell Liza as much!"

"I am... *very* confused," I said blankly, rubbing my eyes and wondering if this was some weird dream.

"I imagine this might be a little confusing, yes, but fear not, your dear old Aunt Constance will straighten out everything for you. Take this, he's yours now!" Constance threw something through the air, and I caught it. It was a small ring with a black gem in the shape of a cat. "Where's Hermes. Is he around here?"

"Right here," a small voice came from the door. Looking over I saw the little black cat sitting in the open doorframe.

"That cat just talked," I said, pointing at Hermes.

"I can sing too if you like," Hermes responded.

I was now talking to a ghost and a cat. "I've officially gone mad."

"Hey, all the women in this family are mad," Constance said lightheartedly. "Poor old Hermes, the little darling hasn't been able to say a word since I died. Stricken with grief he was," Constance said, her hands clasped together.

"Yeah, nothing to do with our spirits being tethered or anything," he said and rolled his eyes.

"What's this ring?" I asked, turning it over and studying it.

"Symbolic ownership of Hermes," Constance explained. "He's yours now, and as such he can talk again."

"Once again I'm feeling confused," I said slowly.

"It's pretty straightforward," Hermes yawned. "When Constance died, I lost my ability to talk. It's not common but it happens with some familiars, especially when they've been around their witches for a long time. Since no one else around here can see ghosts she hasn't been able to talk. Now you're here though, she can pass ownership of me to you, and now I can talk again!"

"Marvelous, right?!" Constance beamed. She was bringing a level of enthusiasm that I wasn't sure I could match right now.

"Why did you wait until now to show yourself?" I asked.

"Well, this is the first time you've been alone," Constance said. "It's much easier for a ghost to appear in front of one person. Now I've got someone to talk to I can probably start building my strength."

"Right..." I said, trying to wrap my head around all of this still. "So, are you going to explain what I'm doing here? Liza said you were secretly in touch with my dad all these years. What do you know about my mom? What happened to—"

"I can see you have a lot of questions, and that's perfectly understandable. Let me answer as succinctly as I can, because we have a lot to go over and to be honest... you look pretty tired."

"Just a little."

"Your father was the one to contact me first. It was in secret, all those years ago. Your mother, Tabatha, my sister, had been traveling across the country on a gap year and fallen pregnant with you during that time. If there's one thing you should know about Tabatha it's this... she always struggled to keep her ducks in a row."

"Meaning?" I asked.

"She was crazier than a snake's armpit," Hermes said flatly. Constance shot him a disapproving glare. "What, she was?!"

Constance rolled her eyes and looked back at me. "It's true that Tabatha had some issues that she was working through. Anyway, while she was traveling the states by herself, she had you in secret with your father. None of us knew about that. I only found out a year after you were born when your father wrote to me in secret."

"What did he say?"

"He said the birth had been fine, but after that the stress had gotten to your mother. When they first got together, I think he knew she was a free spirit, but he underestimated the problems she was facing. Her condition rapidly declined, and she agreed to be hospitalized for her own protection."

"I had no idea; Dad never said anything bad about Mom like that."

"Your father was a good man; he wasn't the type to talk people down. Anyway, the plan was for Tabatha to eventually come back to you and your father, but she disappeared."

"She disappeared?" I asked.

"Disappeared," Constance nodded. "She was locked away in a secure mental health facility and vanished in the dead of night. That same night she appeared halfway across the country, back in Compass Cove."

"So, magic had something to do with it."

"It would seem so but teleporting halfway across the country like that is pretty unheard of and would require an unbelievable amount of magic. To this day I still don't know what happened. Tabatha never said anything about you or your father, but she was suspicious of everyone *and* paranoid. Something wasn't right. Two years after that she had your little sister, Zelda, with that Brewer boy, and not long after that Tabatha disappeared again. No one's ever seen her since."

I sat in silence for a moment as I took in Constance's story. "And no one knows what happened, why she kept vanishing?"

"No one knows a thing," Constance said. "There's theories, but Tabatha was always gifted in unusual magic. I think she got into something she couldn't control."

"And now she's dead..." I said, feeling a little sadness for this woman I had never known.

"I'm not sure myself. Her ghost would have come to visit me. Though we had our own lives we were still close. Tabatha wouldn't have passed up a chance to torment me on her deathday."

"Deathday?"

"The anniversary of a person's death. There are two moments each year when a ghost can reach out to the living, the ones that don't have the ghost sight like yourself: Halloween, and the day of their death. That's how I finally got this ball rolling. I wasted Halloween, still wasn't used to my ghost body, but I was ready on the anniversary of my death. I came to Liza in a dream and showed her where I had hidden the secret letters from your father."

"And now I'm here."

"And now you're here. Which brings us to why I brought you here. There are two reasons. First let me tell you this. In the afterlife you learn things, you get a feel for things. You don't know what's going to happen in the future, but you get a feeling for how things are supposed to be."

"Okay?" I asked, waiting for Constance to explain what that meant.

"Zelda already told you I've been keeping people away from this place. After I died Celeste and Sabrina wanted to take over, look after their momma's bakery. Of course they did! But I knew different. I felt something in my bones..." Constance paused and looked at her transparent hands. "My *spirit*. If Celeste, Sabrina, or Zelda tried to take over this bakery it wouldn't end well. In fact, the feeling I got was so bad I knew I had to keep them away."

"That's why you've been throwing pans at people?" I asked. "Because you think something bad will happen to them if they take over the bakery?"

Constance nodded. "*Exactly*. But I could always see the person that was meant to take over this place. *You*."

"Me?!" I said in startlement. "I could burn cereal… and I have!"

"Forget about that. You just need to learn. Trust me, you're the one that has to take over this place. That's the first reason I brought you here."

"Right… that's… jeez that's a lot to take in."

Constance just laughed. "Well hold onto those bedsheets, darling, because I saved the best for last."

I took a steadying breath, wondering how she could possibly top the first reveal. "Alright, shoot; let's hear it. Why else did you bring me here?"

The translucent blue specter of my departed Aunt leaned in. "Everyone thinks I just up and died. Snuck one too many cakes over the years, clogged my arteries and my ticker stopped tocking."

"You're saying you didn't die of a heart attack?"

"No, darling, I didn't. I was fit as a fiddle. Never been so healthy in my life."

"So how did you die?" I asked.

"Well, this is the part where you come in," Constance said with a knowing smile. "Someone murdered me."

"Murdered?!"

"You bet ya, and here's the cherry on the top. *You're* going to figure out what happened."

* * *

Constance must have been a torturer in her former life, because as soon as she dropped that little nugget of information she floated away through the wall, leaving me alone with Hermes.

"She's seriously just going to leave at that point?"

"You *do* look tired," Hermes said, taking her side. "Besides, Constance always had a theatrical flair; she's not lost it now she's dead. If anything, it's gotten worse. Do you know I've been the only one that could see her this past year? She was the only company I had really. Zelda's not been any use, she barely knew how to translate my meows, but I must say you picked it up pretty well, not that you'll have to do much of that now, I'm back on my feet and singing for England baby, now—Hey! Why did you turn the light off?!"

"Dude, it's after midnight and I spent the last four nights sleeping in a poky rental car. I'm exhausted." Not that I was sure I could even fall asleep after that reveal. In the darkness I felt a little weight jump onto the bed.

"I can always talk you to sleep you know? I thought you'd be a little more impressed with a talking cat; no one else around here finds me interesting. Just wait until Zelda gets here tomorrow, I'm going to talk so much her ears will fall off. Twelve full months I've been subjected to her rehearsals, I don't know why she thought this was an appropriate venue to practice lines for a part she'll never audition for!"

"Zelda does that a lot?" I asked sleepily. I kind of assumed her reading the lines was a one-time thing. Now I knew it was a frequent habit I felt even more sorry for her.

"Let me tell you something, Zora. It's your little sister's dream of being on the stage, but the day she plucks up the courage to actually go and audition is the day I smile at a dog!"

"Why is she so shy?" I asked. "Did something happen to her?"

"Same thing that happened to you, I guess. Grew up without a real mother, but from the sounds of things your father was a decent guy, Billy Brewer on the other hand—"

"He hurt her?"

"Nah, nothing like that, but he wasn't exactly winning any awards for father of the year. The Brewers aren't exactly the type to do sentimental love. Zelda's family is here, with Constance and her cousins. I think Zelda always had it in her head that she was a burden."

"That's ridiculous, she was a child when my mom disappeared."

"The thing you have to understand about Zelda is that she's very socially intelligent, always has been. She puts a lot of effort into caring about other people's feelings, sometimes perhaps a little too much. Constance was always supportive growing up, but you know how it is, some people just have a hard time coming out of that shell."

"I get it," I said. For the longest time I'd been the shy kid myself. In some ways I still was, but I'd learned that getting by in this world meant you couldn't be timid. You had to fight for what you believed in. "I'm in her corner now. I'll put her right."

Hermes just laughed back at me in the darkness. "You're a bad influence, I can already see it, but hey, I'm looking forward to someone shaking things up around here. This town could use some new blood!"

"I'm falling asleep now," I said, my eyes beginning to lull heavily.

"I'm going to go and watch old cowboy movies on the TV. Sweet dreams!"

I WOKE up the next morning and for a few seconds the events of the night before escaped me. As I got out of bed it all came rushing back to me. I was a witch, my aunt was a ghost, I'd just adopted a cat that could talk.

There was a good chance I'd gone off the road on the drive across the country, wrapped my car around an eighteen-wheeler, and fallen into a deep coma. None of this was real and it was all some elaborate daydream conjured up by an oxygen starved brain. Maybe I was strapped to a hospital bed, wires and tubes coming out of me while machines beeped all around.

Walking into the main apartment I saw Hermes passed out on the couch, the TV still on, playing the end of some old John Wayne movie. I went over and turned it off. Hermes stretched and sat up on the couch.

"Sleep well?" he asked. "You look all spacey."

"I'm wondering if any of this is real," I said. "A week ago, I was working this crumby zero-hour contract job, living in a shoebox in a rat-infested city."

"Oh, we got rats here, big ones. Just the other night one of them tried to take me back to its rat nest and feed me to its children. I had to fight it off with my claws."

I stared at Hermes for a second. "Does everyone make up stories around here?"

"That's not a story; it actually happened! Thank you very much!"

"I'm just adjusting to all this still. It's been a lot of change and I feel dizzy. First, I find out I'm a witch, then I find I have a sister. *Then* Constance floats through my wall, tells me she wants me to take over her café and avenge her death!"

"Bakery," Constance said as she floated through the wall in front of me. I jumped out of my skin and put my hand against my heart.

"What?! Can you not sneak up on me like that!"

"It's a bakery, not a café, and you'll do a fine job of taking the reins, I just know it. You just need a little guidance."

"I'll tell you what I need less of: big grand reveals three minutes before I go to bed."

Constance opened her mouth to argue back but stopped herself. "I suppose that's fair. I'll keep the real identity of D.B Cooper to myself then."

"You don't…" I said, wondering if she actually knew. "Forget it, I'm not falling for it. I need to go and get breakfast somewhere, and then make a plan for the day."

"Why do you need to go and get breakfast?" she asked. "Why not make it yourself?"

"I don't know if you heard me last night over your grandstanding, but I'm not inclined in the ways of making food. I can heat up a mean can of soup, but my culinary expertise stops there."

"Well, let us make breakfast then. This is the perfect opportunity for you to learn! What do you want, pancakes?"

"Pancakes? I could go for some pancakes right about now."

"Brilliant. Meet me in the kitchen downstairs." Without another word Constance floated through the floor and vanished. I sighed and looked at Hermes.

"She's not going to stop doing that, is she?"

"Hey it saves time. Would you take the stairs if you could float through walls?"

"Oh, stop taking her side, what do you know anyway, you're a cat!"

"*Meow,*" Hermes said, actually saying the word instead of making the sound. It was laced in sarcasm. "I'm not the only one here with claws!"

CHAPTER 8

Downstairs I found the bakery kitchen was sparkling clean, which was nothing short of a miracle considering how it looked after the fire extinguisher yesterday.

"Holy ham joint, did you do all this?" I asked, looking at Constance's floating ghost.

"Yes, and let me make something clear, it won't happen again. From now on this kitchen is your responsibility. I cleaned up as way of thanks."

"Thanks, thanks for what?"

"For that hilarious first encounter you had with Zelda. I was watching the entire time; I haven't laughed that hard in a year!"

"You're welcome I guess," I mumbled under my breath. Looking around the kitchen I felt a little intimidated. There was a whole host of equipment in here, and I didn't know what half of it did. "Are you really sure you want to entrust your bakery business to me? I wasn't joking earlier when I said I burned cereal once. I had to throw the bowl out."

"The first step to being good at something is kind of sucking at something. I read that on a toilet seat once."

"Wait, an actual toilet seat?"

"Yes, I wouldn't pick it personally, but the quote stuck with me. Grab an apron; they're on the wall behind you."

Turning around, I grabbed an apron off the wall and tied it around my body. "I just feel like we need to get our priorities in order a little," I said, trying to stall for time a little further. "Last night you told me you think you were murdered. I feel like that takes precedence over learning to make pancakes."

"First of all," Constance said, putting one ghostly hand on the table and another in the air. "I don't think I was murdered. I *was* murdered. Second of all, you come from a long line of kitchen witches. This is in your blood. You can do this. I know you can. The act of making food alone will charge your magic and inform your learning. We start here."

"Can't you even give me any hints as to why you think— I mean, why you *were* murdered?" Constance smiled. "What?"

"I knew you'd be interested. Your father mentioned in those letters you studied investigative journalism at college. He even mentioned how you helped uncover that scholarship fraud."

"He really told you all that?" I said. Dad had always been supportive of me, but I never knew he went around talking about me to others.

"Oh, he gushed about you, darling. You've clearly got a knack for things; you just have to believe in yourself a little."

I heard someone snort on the stairs behind me and turned to see Hermes sitting in the doorway. "What are you laughing at?" I asked.

"Oh nothing, just sounds mighty similar to the pep talk you were giving to Zelda earlier. You guys are more alike than you realize."

I went to argue but had to admit that Hermes had a pretty good point. Maybe magic and baking really was just as easy as believing in myself—to begin with anyway.

"How about we make a deal," Constance said. "You cook up a decent batch of pancakes, and we'll talk about the murder."

"Well, how's a girl supposed to resist an offer like that?" I joked. "Let's start. Where's the cookbook?"

"Lesson number one. Your cookbook is in here," Constance said, pointing at her heart.

"Are we about to have a kumbaya moment?" I asked. Constance flicked her hand in response and a pan came whizzing across the room, right at my face. I ducked under it, and it clattered to the floor behind me.

"Any more funny jokes?" she said with a raised brow.

"I thought you were one of those cool aunt types…" I muttered under my breath.

"Oh, that was regular Constance," Hermes said from his doorway. "This is kitchen Constance. You don't mess with kitchen Constance. That's lesson two."

"Received loud and clear," I said, looking back at Constance. "Go ahead. No more interruptions from these sassy pants."

"You're a kitchen witch," Constance reiterated. "You don't need cookbooks. You don't need guides. Everything you need to know is already inside you. Don't think, tell me straight away. What goes in pancakes?"

"Flour, eggs, milk, salt!" I said quickly, giving the answer rapid-fire. It wasn't exactly a complicated answer, but I'd never made pancakes in my life, so I wondered where the words had come from. "Wait, is that right?" I asked in astonishment.

"Absolutely, because you used your intuition. Let me guess, every time you tried to cook in the past you relied on instruction, squinting at tiny writing on packets, or some kooky food blog?"

"Well yeah, how else am I supposed to do it?"

"And let me guess, every time you did that it ended horribly."

"Need I repeat that I burned cereal?"

"I fully believe you did. You probably didn't realize it at that time, but those things went horribly wrong because your magic was trying to interfere. It was telling you, *stop, we've got this,* but you've been pushing that voice down. No longer!" she said, pointing at the ceiling with dramatic flair.

"Okay… so I've got ingredients, but I haven't got amounts, and I don't know where anything is—wait, what are you doing?" I asked, preparing to duck out of the way as I saw Constance pick up a kitchen timer.

"You have five minutes," she said. "When the timer goes off, I expect a plate of perfect pancakes in front of me. You will receive no more instruction from me. Remember, everything you need is already..." She pointed at her chest. "Here. Go!"

Constance twisted the timer to five minutes and slammed it down on the table. I immediately fell into panic mode, turning around on the spot as I tried to find the basic utensils and ingredients to make pancakes.

The next five minutes was a confusing blur of frantic chaos. At the start I was throwing open drawers and cabinets desperately, determined to try and rise to the impossible challenge in the short time frame. I had no quantities, no list of ingredients, just this vague sense of mounting doubt that I was doing everything wrong.

I was panicking so much that I dropped one of the metal cups I had found halfway through scooping flour. I bent down to grab it from under the counter when I saw one of the sheets from the play Zelda had been rehearsing from. I picked it up, stood up slowly, and set it down.

From that point it was like a switch flipped in me. Hermes was right. Yesterday I told Zelda she needed to believe in herself, and now —perhaps hypocritically—I couldn't do the same thing for myself. It was just pancakes for gosh sake, how hard could it be?

"Right, let's do this," I whispered determinedly to myself, turning back to the island in the middle of the kitchen and facing my ingredients. Somehow it was different then. I knew how much milk I needed to splash into the bowl, I knew exactly how much flour to sift, and I knew how many eggs I needed as well. I mixed it all up, fired up a burner on the stove and added a little oil to a large pan that was so heavy my forearms burned just from picking it up. I found a spatula in the first drawer I opened, and I poured batter into the hot pan.

When the timer buzzed, I had just finished placing the last pancake onto the plate. I collapsed onto my knees in breathlessness, holding my hands against the counter, pressing my forehead against the edge.

"Done!" I panted. It felt like I'd just run a marathon.

"Excellent," Constance said. It was the first word she had uttered since setting the timer five minutes ago. The brief slot of time simultaneously felt like a lifetime and a snap of the fingers. "Stand up, time to do a taste test. I must admit they look pretty good. You were panicking at the start, but you got a hold of yourself."

I stood up and saw Constance holding a fork in my direction. "Aren't you going to try them?" I asked.

"Uh, hello? Ghost, remember? You're the judge, jury, and executioner."

I took the fork, cut a little triangle piece of pancake, and put it in my mouth. "Oh my god; it's amazing," I said through the mouthful of pancake.

Constance smiled. "Then it looks like you passed the test. It seems you have it in you after all."

"Rule number three," Hermes said from the doorway. "I always get scraps." I took one of the pancakes off the plate and frisbeed it towards the cat. His eyes lit up. "I like her!" he said to Constance before picking up the pancake in his mouth and running out of the kitchen.

"So, I really did a good job?" I asked Constance.

"Looks like it," she said with a smile. "Hermes is just about the harshest critic I know. If you get a thumbs-up from him then it's a thumbs-up from me."

"Do cats have thumbs?"

"Metaphorically speaking, yes. Now there's a few things you could have done differently to make your life a bit easier, but I'll put that down to your panic at the start. There's a small griddle on the counter behind you for instance. Easier to use than a pan, and it lets you cook batches faster. Also use the batter gun next time, it gives you an even distribution of batter and you can make them all identical sizes."

Before Constance mentioned either of these things, I'd felt like I could improve my method. I'd already been eyeing up that griddle, and the batter gun on the countertop next to it.

"Pancakes aren't really a staple item on a bakery menu, are they?" I asked.

"No, they're not, but it's a good starter. In the world of professional baking, cakes and tray bakes are your best friends. You have everything you need in this kitchen to be back in business before the end of the week. The rest is up to you."

"You're kidding!" I said in alarm. "I've only just mastered pancakes; I can't open a bakery by the end of the week!"

Constance just rolled her eyes. "Belief, remember? That's the most important tool in your business plan. Without it you *will* fail. Magic is ninety-nine percent fed from imagination and intent. If you're trying to achieve something, then imagine the end goal and work backwards from there."

"Pretty good advice," I grumbled. I looked at the door leading into the bakery, a room I still hadn't actually ventured into. "I suppose I should look inside there if I'm really going to do this." I headed over to the door and paused, glancing back at Constance. "You're not going to throw a pan at me, are you?"

Constance laughed. "Only if you step out of line."

I opened the door and headed into the dark and dusty room. Through the windows at the front of the shop I could see the street outside brightening with morning sunlight. I walked into the middle of the room and stood there. There were half a dozen tables in all, a thick coating of dust covering every available surface.

I let my eyes wander around the dark room, trying to imagine what things might look like if the bakery was back up and running. My imagination had always been pretty strong, but in that moment, it was like I had stepped through a portal into another world.

The bakery lit up, its bright lights turning on overhead and the glass counters illuminating to show shelves full of different baked goods. All around me the room was alive with the sound of chatter and laughter, coming from customers sitting around the tables. Behind the counter I saw myself in a pink and white apron, quickly moving about at the register while I took an order form another customer.

"*Daphne!*" the vision version of myself shouted. "*We need another batch of scones, pronto!*"

"*Coming right up!*" someone responded from the back.

I stepped forward to see more, but the bright image faded from view, like water running down a drain. Once again, I was back in the bakery, but this time the dark and dusty version. I saw Constance leaning in the door, her arms crossed while she watched me.

"Already performing magic, I see," she commented.

"I was just daydreaming. It's been a bad habit all my life."

"No, it's your magic, trying to express itself. That wasn't a daydream; it was a vision of what could happen if you put yourself to it. It felt real, didn't it?"

I nodded. The vision had felt more like a memory, like I could have reached forward and touched something. "So, what do I do now?"

Constance held her hands up as if she didn't know the answer. "Hey, this is your bakery now. If you want this to work, you have to figure it out. Things will be better that way."

"So, we're really going with the tough love approach, eh?"

"You know it, sister!" she said with a wink.

Chuckling, I rolled my eyes and headed back into the bakery kitchen. "I guess that brings us to our next big-ticket item then. Why are you so sure you were murdered?"

Constance broke out in a big grin. "I was starting to think you'd never ask. Take a seat."

I sat in a chair at the main island as Constance disappeared through the ceiling. She came back a moment later, this time coming down the stairs and through the open door. Constance floated over and set two things down on the counter in front of me, a small pot with a trace of white powder in it, and a newspaper with the headline, 'Local Baker Found Dead'.

The newspaper seemed self-explanatory, but I had no idea what the white powder was. "What is this?" I asked, picking up the pot.

"I don't know, but that's the thing that killed me. I found that underneath one of the counters in my kitchen a couple of days after I died. It's not mine, and no one else ever came back here. I think my killer was in here, and I think they dropped it."

"Wait a second, you don't remember?"

"The last twenty-four hours of my life are a haze. I think it happens to everyone upon passing. It's supposed to protect the soul in case anything super tragic happened to you. The paper says I had a heart attack; they found me in the alleyway behind the bakery."

"What were you doing out there?"

Constance shrugged. "I have no idea. Apart from the heart attack there were no other clues as to what happened to me. No struggle, no wounds. It looks like maybe I was running to get help."

"So, I have two clues to go off."

"Oh, three actually!" she said quickly. "I have *one* memory, a very vague recollection being in the park at nighttime."

"A usual haunt for you?" I queried.

"What do I look like, the girl that dies first in every horror movie? I wasn't one to habitually visit a park at nighttime."

My brain set to ticking, however. "Consider my curiosity piqued. Your apartment looks right over the park, doesn't it?"

"It does. Do you think that memory has something to do with my death? You have this look in your eye. It's quite inspiring!"

I shrugged. "I don't know what I think yet, but it couldn't hurt to check out the park, maybe jog your memory. Plus, I've not been there yet myself. I'll go and get dressed upstairs, then we can check things out."

"You really think you can solve this?" Constance asked.

"Hey, it can't hurt to try," I said and ran upstairs.

CHAPTER 9

Once I was dressed and ready to go, I headed across the street in the direction of the park. Constance was floating alongside as I walked, only visible to me.

"I can't tell you how good it feels to finally have someone working on this!" she said excitedly as we entered the park. I was taken back by how large the green space was. It seemed that Compass Cove town had its own little garden of Eden, hidden away only a few blocks from the town center.

"It's gorgeous here!" I remarked as we followed a path through the park. Trees bordered the park on all sides, and a large, luscious field of grass ran throughout the rest of the area. "A great lunch spot."

"Yes, it's quite handy being so close to the bakery. A lot of the tourists come to the park naturally, so the bakery used to pick up quite a lot of the foot traffic."

"Does this town really get that many tourists?" I asked. "I mean no offense, but it's not exactly the Big Apple."

Constance laughed. "It receives a surprising amount of attention. Compass Cove in itself brings a lot of tourism in the summer; it's a great spot for fishing and water sports. The next nearest waterfront is two hours or so away from here."

"I guess I hadn't thought of that."

"It's quite the draw, but the cove isn't the only reason people come here. The flight center brings in all the space nuts," Constance explained.

"I met a guy that works there actually; he was in the information center yesterday. I bet the flight center stuff brings in the UFO nuts too."

"Not so much the flight center, but the military base a few miles outside of town certainly does."

"There's a military base around here?" I asked with a note of interest. A woman walking by with her dog gave me an odd glance and I realized it looked like I was talking to myself. I pulled out my phone and held it to my ear, pretending I was on a call.

Constance shook her head and laughed at my cover. "There is, and from the rumors they've got some weird stuff going on up there. Local legends say a UFO crashed here back in the seventies, but a lot of people were doing acid back then so who's to say what's the truth."

"Never seen one myself."

"Go camping around here and you'll trip over them, sightings at least. I've lost count of how many weird lights I've seen in the sky around here at night."

"Could it have something to do with magic?" I asked.

"I don't think so. A witch can feel out other magical sources, you'll learn that. Do it now. Look at me and you'll feel a slight vibration in your fingertips." I did look at her, and sure enough I felt my fingertips vibrate ever so slightly.

"What's that about?" I asked.

"You're feeling the magic. If you actively look for it with your mind you can feel it. That's how you can tell whether another person is a witch or not. Over time you'll hone that feeling and it will become second nature."

I guess I still had a lot to learn about magic. "So why else do people come to this town?"

"The architecture draws a lot of folks in. They also filmed that TV show here in the eighties, *Mysterious Encounters*."

"Oh, I loved that show! Is that why the town feels so familiar?!" Growing up it was a weekly ritual for me and my dad to watch Mysterious Encounters on Wednesday nights. The show followed two 'paranormal agents' solving mysterious encounters and unusual murders. It was a little after my bedtime, but Dad always let me stay up late to watch it with him.

"Could be one of the reasons. The show has a cult following to this day, and we still get a lot of visitors off the back of it, even though it hasn't aired for the better part of two decades."

"They still show reruns daily though. Sometimes I watch it in the afternoon on weekends." It was like stepping into a time machine and going back to a point in my life when it was just me and Dad. No bills, no job, no worries—beyond the usual teenage troubles.

"I must admit I'm partial to an episode here and there too," Constance said with a wink. "That male agent isn't hard on the eyes either!"

"Sounds like there are plenty of reasons for people to visit the town then," I surmised.

"Oh yes, and that's not even accounting for the many films that have been shot here over the years. Those Hollywood types love the vintage look of the town. People also come for the weekend markets too. You've probably noticed there are a lot of small businesses here. Tourists love the artisanal selection in Compass Cove. There are even hot springs up in the mountains."

"This place really does have everything."

"Yes, I hope you love it here, Zora; I know I did," Constance said with a note of sadness. Looking over I saw her expression and pulled myself back to the mission at hand. Constance believed she was murdered, someone had to do something about that.

"Okay," I said, stopping on the path. We had walked one entire length of the park now, looking back in the direction we came from. There were several shallow decorative pools and fountains in front of us, spouts of water dancing rhythmically through the air. "You have a memory of being in the park at nighttime."

"That's right," Constance said.

I looked around the park, wondering why Constance would have a memory of that, especially as she said she never went to the park at night. "You think you had a heart attack in the bakery and then tried to head outside to the back alley for help."

"I assume that's what happened. Why else would I be out there?"

"What if something happened to you in the park. You started struggling there and *then* made your way to the alley behind the shop."

Constance blinked as though she'd never considered that before. "Why, that's definitely another way of looking at things. That would explain the hazy memory."

"But why would you be in the park, especially at that time of night?" I asked.

Just then I heard a chorus of thunder. I looked up to the sky, thinking another storm was about to break out, but I realized rather quickly the sound came from the other end of the park. There I saw a group of bikers pull into the park and turn off their bikes.

"Those bikers," Constance growled through gritted teeth.

"You know those guys?" I said in surprise.

"I don't know them, but I'm familiar with them. They started coming to the park about a year and a half ago to deal drugs. Mostly they keep to themselves, but their bikes cause a real racket, and they definitely put everyone else on edge."

"Why don't the police do anything about it?" I asked.

"Oh, that's the question of the hour right there!" Constance scoffed. "I've lost count of how many times I brought it up. They're just bikers, but they're smart. They don't do anything out in the open. As far as scumbags go, they're quite sophisticated."

"I didn't think an idyllic little town like Compass Cove would have drug dealers."

"We're not exactly overflowing with crime, but ever since these guys moved in things haven't felt right. I hope someone can get them out before more trouble shows up, but alas… they haven't gone yet."

"I'm going to talk to them," I said after a moment of consideration.

"Are you crazy?!" Constance balked. "They're criminals, murderers!"

"I interviewed a biker once when I was in college. I even went for a drink at his gang's bar."

"You really are crazy," Constance said, though she seemed impressed.

"I was actually gunning for the extra credit. I'd failed an earlier module because I was working so much to pay the bills, so I had to catch up. Anyway, I interviewed this biker and went to the bar. It wasn't that bad; everyone was very courteous. A lot of them offered me drinks."

"I bet they did. But not every bike gang out there is like that, Zora. Some of these guys are real criminals, like the guys standing over there."

"Here's what I've ascertained so far, Constance. You said there's not really any crime in Compass Cove."

"Correct."

"These guys only moved in here recently, and there's no other gang presence."

"That's right."

"So, we now know two things. These guys are here because no one else is, and from what you say the territory can't be that profitable because most of the people in this town don't do drugs. We can infer then that they're not out fighting over some more profitable corner in a real city because they've still got their training wheels on."

"You're calling those roughnecks a bunch of babies?!" she laughed.

I shrugged. "That's my going theory, and I guess there's only one way to test it. Besides, you said they're here *all* the time. Who better to speak to as a witness?"

"I suppose you've got a fair point…" Constance said, hurrying after me as I started walking. "Just be careful though! If these guys really are d-list bikers like you assume then they can still be a threat. Nothing is more dangerous than a man with something to prove."

"Amen to that," I said as I walked over.

Admittedly I was a little nervous walking over to the four men. They were all big, and the choppers behind them were even bigger. I felt grateful to have Constance by my side, even if no one else could see her.

The bikers took notice of me as I got closer, muttering to one another and nodding in my direction. I recognized one of them right away as the jerk wad that had been in Celeste's café yesterday.

"Morning," I said as I walked up to them. The four of them looked back at me for a moment.

"Well, well," the jerk said first, his lips curling into an insidious smile. "Look who came crawling back. You want that number after all, baby?"

"I'm actually here on other business," I said. "I'm a journalist, and I'm looking into the death of a woman that took place here a year ago. She owned the bakery over the road; her name was Constance Wick. Did any of you know her?"

The jerk stepped forward, eager to show off in front of his friends. The other bikers all looked a little older and hadn't really reacted so far, other than passing glances. "If you're looking for a lead then I've got one for you right here in my pants," the jerk said and winked.

"Nick, go to the store and get some sandwiches," one of the bikers said from the rear.

"Hey, I'm talking to the—"

"Go," the same biker snarled. 'Nick' swallowed and shook his head.

"Whatever." He looked back at me. "I'll see you around, darling," he said and walked off in the direction of the street. The biker that dismissed him looked at the other two and made some sort of motion with his head. They nodded and he walked towards me.

As he came closer, I realized for the first time just how good-looking he was. He was tall, handsome, with dark hair, large brown eyes, a square jaw and thick brown hair. He looked more like a model pretending to be a biker than an actual biker.

"I'll talk to you. Two minutes on the bench over there. You're scaring away business," he said, pointing at a bench just down the path. He walked over without waiting for a response and I followed.

The biker sat down at one end of the bench, and I sat down at the other, leaving quite a gap between us. For a second, I just found myself staring at his near-perfect profile. He turned and looked at me with his sharp eyes. My stomach dropped and I laughed nervously before stopping myself.

"So, uh… what was that little head motion you made to your friends back there?" I asked.

"That was code for, 'Don't worry I'll get her out of the way,'" he said coolly.

"Sorry to inconvenience your fine business of selling drugs," I replied.

"Was there something you wanted to talk about?" he asked, reminding me in a not-so-subtle way.

"Constance Wick," I repeated. "She died near here just over a year ago, and I'm looking into it. Massive heart attack, late at night."

"Why do you think we'd know anything about that?" he asked.

"You just brought me over here to talk," I pointed out.

"I already told you I was getting you out of the way." He said the words calmly, throwing in a smile at the end that would make my knees weak if I wasn't already sitting down. He was irritatingly confident, and kind of arrogant too, but I'd be damned if I said he wasn't attractive.

"You don't know anything then?"

"If I did, I probably wouldn't talk to you anyway. My kind don't really talk, especially to lousy undercover cops."

I laughed at the accusation. "I am not a cop!"

"Well, you've got all the makings of one. I don't know many pretty white girls that would march up to a biker gang without good reason."

Pretty. Pretty. Oh god he said pretty. "It's even more dangerous when you take into account that I'm single!" I blurted out.

"What?" he asked, confused and amused.

"Uh, what?" I couldn't believe my brain actually tricked my mouth into blurting that one out. "I'm not a cop, I promise."

"Well now I've got your scout's honor I'll start singing like a bird," he said sarcastically. "What paper are you with?"

"I'm… freelance at the moment."

Hot biker guy laughed. "You're really painting a convincing picture here."

I let out a frustrated breath and pushed my fingers through my hair. "Okay, I'm not a freelance journalist. I mean, I have a degree in journalism, but I'm not covering a story or anything. The woman that died was my aunt, and I have reason to believe she was murdered. My name is Zora Wick."

The biker suddenly looked at me, a querying expression on his face. "I remember reading about some woman being found in an alleyway around a year ago. Is that her? They said it was a heart attack."

"That's what they said, but I have reason to believe different. Listen I hear you guys are here all hours of the day, is there any chance you heard or saw something?"

"No," he said after thinking about it for a moment. His hesitation seemed suspicious. "What makes you think she was murdered?"

"I found something in her kitchen, a small pot of white powder. She claims—I mean, her daughter claims it didn't belong to her mother."

His intrigue grew at mention of the powder. "You think this powder killed her?"

"Possibly. It could have been left at the scene of the crime by the murderer."

"And where is it now, somewhere safe?"

"Who are you, my father?"

"I'm just saying, if I had a deadly substance like that in my belonging, I'd be really careful with it."

"Thanks for the pep talk, chief," I said, wondering why I was getting a lecture from an outlaw biker of all people. "You don't know anything then?"

"Nope, and even if I did—"

"Yeah, yeah, you wouldn't say anything. I get it. Well thanks for nothing," I said, standing up to leave. As I walked past him the biker called out.

"Hey, Zora, right?" he asked. I looked back at him and nodded. "In my line of work it's important to have contacts, professional people that can help you without asking questions. There's a pharmacist on Dixon Street, his name is Colin. Take your powder to him, he'll be able to tell you what it is."

"Uh… thanks," I said. "What happened to not knowing anything?"

Hot biker guy shrugged and put on a pair of shades. "Hey, you didn't hear it from me." He stood up and went to walk back to his accomplices. "My name's Hudson by the way. See you around, Zora."

CHAPTER 10

"How good-looking are we talking here?" Zelda asked while sipping tea at the kitchen table in Constance's apartment. "Like, cute guy on the bus, or California Reaper hot?"

"Both of those mashed together, and then multiply by a hundred. Tall, dark, mysterious—"

"And a criminal outlaw," Hermes added between mouthfuls of cat food.

"That as well," I said with a conceding nod.

"That adds to the romance, Hermes," Zelda explained. "You wouldn't understand, being a cat and all, and a male one at that."

"Just so we're all on the same page here," Hermes said while lifting his head. "The element of possibly being murdered by someone makes them hotter?"

"The heart wants what it wants," I sang.

"No one ever said love makes sense," Zelda added with a giggle.

After finishing her morning shift at the café Zelda came over to the apartment. I caught her up to speed with everything that had happened since she left, and we'd basically been talking nonstop for two and a half hours. I told her everything, from Constance showing up, to her suspicion of being murdered, to my run-in with the bikers at the park.

I didn't even look at the time for the first hour. Being with Zelda was fun and effortless, and if I was being honest, I kind of loved having a sister, someone I could always talk to. We had the same sense of humor and a similar outlook, we got on so well it was like we'd always known each other.

"Gosh," Constance said as she floated through the floor. "Y'all are still talking? I've been around the cove and back again."

"Constance is here," I said to Zelda as a heads-up. The pair of them had an impromptu catch-up through me when Zelda first got here, but it was a little difficult for them to talk properly as Zelda couldn't see or hear Constance, so I had to relay everything back to her.

"Where's she been?" Zelda asked.

"Tell her I was on my daily lap around the cove. I do it every day; it takes me an hour to float around."

"She's been spying on naked guys down at the gym," I said with a smirk.

"Zora!" Constance said in horror.

"I totally buy it," Zelda laughed. "Constance was always a dark horse. Have you told her about your criminal lover?"

"She was there, she saw the whole thing," I reminded Zelda.

Constance floated over to the table and sat down. "I saw the whole thing, Zelda; it was incredibly embarrassing. Zora can't flirt to save her life; the biker is a hottie though."

Zelda saw me staring at the spot where Constance was sitting. "What did she say?"

"She said I handled the situation with deft and grace. Women could learn a thing or two from my flirting skills."

Zelda almost spit up her tea. "*Now* I know you're lying."

Constance rolled her eyes. "If you're going to sit here and twist all my words I'll just go!"

"I'm only kidding, calm down, you old cougar. I bet you've snuck down to that gym to peep the changing rooms at some point in the last year."

Constance looked left to right and scratched her neck. "Is that the time already? I should really go and check on Celeste and Sabrina and make sure they're okay." With that, Constance disappeared through the wall.

"What did she say?" Zelda asked after another moment of watching me.

"She's totally been creeping on naked guys. Rumor confirmed."

Zelda snorted. "I knew it. So, what's your plan now then? Open up the bakery again and solve Constance's murder?"

"Well, that's what Constance wants. She had me make some pancakes earlier and they did turn out pretty well. Hudson has given me a potential lead to get this powder identified, so there's that too."

"Ooh, Hudson. I didn't realize you were on first name basis."

"How about you," I asked. "How's your love life?"

"Oh, you know… nonexistent. There aren't a ton of eligible bachelors around here, not ones I'm interested in anyway."

"She's lying," Hermes said through a mouthful of food.

"Say again, kitty?" I said, turning to face him.

"She's in love," Hermes sang, dragging the words out nice and long. "She's in love with Joshua."

"Ooh Joshua!" I said excitedly. "He sounds like a dream. How handsome is he?"

"Will you shut up?" Zelda whispered through clenched teeth at Hermes. She looked back at me, her cheeks a fluster. "Joshua is just a friend of mine down at the local theatre. He plays the piano there. We're friends. *That's all.*"

"She mutters his name when she naps," Hermes said. "She naps here all the time."

"I do not!" Zelda said defensively. "Besides, I already have a boyfriend."

"You do?" I asked, sitting up slightly in my chair. I had a lot of catching up to do with my little sister, and I wanted to learn as much about her as possible.

"Yawn," Hermes said. "You are not about to mention Gavin—"

"Gavin is very lovely, and you barely know anything about him."

"I know you let him walk all over you, and you could do far better. Someone that isn't a jerk, someone that doesn't ignore you for days on end. Someone like… Joshua!" Hermes darted out of the room as Zelda jumped up to catch him. She didn't move more than a couple of steps from the table; I think she was mostly just trying to shoo him away.

"Hermes is a serial liar. Gavin is my boyfriend, and we're very happy."

"But when I asked you about your love life you said it was nonexistent."

"Ah…" Zelda said, noticing the conflicting answers. She let out a big sigh and rested her head in her hands. "Fine, you've got me. Gavin is not exactly the prince charming I imagined when I was growing up. I should have ended it ages ago, but he always ends up crying and begging me to come back."

"Yuck, already I don't like him," I said. "But hey, you've got a big sis to look out for you now. I've got your back; you can do this. Ditch Gavin and get with Joshua. We'll both get married to our hot soulmates on the same day, ride off into the sunset, and have a thousand babies!"

"Not that your little dream doesn't sound lovely, but Joshua already has a girlfriend, a fiancée in fact. They've been together for two years."

"Aww," I said, deflating a little over this person I didn't even know. "But she's horrible, right? He'd be far better off with you?"

"That's the worst part. She's actually perfectly lovely, so I can't even be upset about it."

"So, you do like him?" I asked, even though it was obvious she did.

Zelda looked around to make sure Hermes was gone but nodded her head sadly. "Yeah, I do. I have for ages actually, like since we were at school together."

"Wowzer," I said, blowing out a mouthful of air. "If it's any consolation my love life hasn't exactly been so hot either." I proceeded to tell Zelda all about my troubles with my ex, Tyler, and the way he'd saddled me with a ton of debt. By the time she'd finished asking me questions about it all I looked up at the clock and saw that it was nearly five. "Blinking heck, Zel, we've nearly been talking for four hours. Should we get some dinner or something?"

"I am definitely down for—oh man, I completely forgot!"

"What?" I said, intrigued by the sudden panic.

"Celeste told me earlier, but I completely blanked on it. Sabrina and Celeste are coming over. Sabrina wants to meet you!"

"When is this happening?"

"In like fifteen minutes!" Zelda grinned sheepishly. "It slipped my mind, sorry!"

"That's alright, as your older sister I get to give you swirlies every time you mess up. It's written in the big sister handbook."

"I'll go and get my shower cap then," Zelda joked back.

After a quick bit of tidying up we opened the door to Celeste and Sabrina. Celeste I had already met once at her café yesterday. Sabrina ran through the door screaming with her arms in the air. She threw them around me and started jumping up and down.

"New cousin, new cousin!" she shouted. I felt like a cat getting pounced by a pack of puppies.

"Meet Sabrina," Celeste said as she pulled her sister off me. "Her spirit animal is a huskie that got into a duffel bag of cocaine."

"I don't do cocaine, or any drugs!" Sabrina looked at me with one brow raised. "My energy comes from the universe and crystals. Lots of crystals." Sabrina looked like a hippie crossed with a skater. She had on a tie-die crop top, large baggy jeans that had to be from the nineties, and white Converse painted with pink cherry blossoms. She scooped a palmful of rose crystals out of her pockets and put them into my hands. "Quartz, relieves stress and anxiety; you'll need it in this family!"

Suddenly Constance's ghostly form appeared through the wall behind her daughters. They didn't yet know why she'd summoned me here.

"Let's head upstairs and have some cake and tea," I said. "It's been a busy twenty-four hours, and I've got a lot to catch you up with."

* * *

"I'm confused," Celeste said as I finished retelling everything that had happened so far. "Do we think hot biker guy knows something about Mom's death?"

"I don't know. He was hiding something from me, that's for sure," I said. "We only really have two clues so far—your mom has hazy memories of the park at night, and she found that small container of mysterious white powder under a cabinet in her kitchen. I'm going to get it tested tomorrow."

"Well hopefully she'll stop throwing pans at us now when we come over," Sabrina said. "That got old fast. We were just trying to keep your business going!"

"Sabrina, you're a green witch, darling, you never could have kept up," Constance said. I relayed that message to Sabrina; I'd been communicating between Constance and her two daughters since they'd come to the bakery. It was a slow and lengthy process.

"What's a green witch?" I added.

"I didn't get the kitchen-witch gene, though I suppose gene is the wrong word. I'm better suited to herbalism, botany, that sort of thing. I grow a lot of the food Celeste uses in her café," Sabrina explained.

"And I'm not much of a baker," Celeste clarified. "I much prefer the savory side of kitchen magic. Don't get me wrong, I love to eat cakes. A girl doesn't get curves like this without an appetite for sugar."

"Mom, why was Zelda the only one you let in here?" Sabrina asked, staring at a blank spot on the wall next to me. Constance had moved to the other end of the table. I pointed in the right direction, and everyone turned their heads to look in the general direction.

"You girls don't understand. It's different in the afterlife. You get a vibe about things. Whenever you and Celeste came around, I got this ominous feeling that something bad would happen if you spent too much time around the bakery. I don't get that with Zelda, or with Zora." Once again, I reiterated the words so everyone could hear.

"If you really think you were murdered, we should get the police involved," Celeste said.

Sabrina just rolled her eyes and scoffed. "Like they'll be any help.

They're already up to their knees trying to get the roads cleared. If we want this solved, then we have to do it ourselves!"

"You once got lost in your own house," Zelda pointed out. "What do you have to offer in this situation?"

"Hey, that was in the basement, and that basement is very confusing… and scary!" Sabrina looked at me and explained. "I have these old wine cellars running under my house. It's very cool, but also kind of creepy. They cover quite a bit of ground."

"Sounds like something out of a horror movie," I said.

"Oh yeah, it's horrible. I never go down there anymore unless I'm storing something. Man, look at the time. I'm starving. Zel, has Zora had the delight of trying Voodoo Pizza yet?"

"No, we had Ping's last night though."

"Ping's! I love Ping's!" Sabrina dropped her head back and closed her eyes. "Let's get pizza though. Lana said she's got this new onion-ring crust and this Italian mayo dressing—"

"Ordering right now, ordering right now," Celeste said and pulled out her phone. "I'm thinking Pizza Fairy."

"Lana's a friend of ours," Zelda explained. "She's a kitchen witch too. She runs this place called Pizza Fairy further down on Main Street. It's really the best pizza you'll ever eat in your life."

"Sign me up!" I said excitedly. If there was one good thing about moving to a new place it was trying all the new food. Before long the pizza arrived and we ate around the table, talking, joking, listening to music, catching up on a lifetime of stories late into the evening.

Rain beat against the windows and the world went dark.

CHAPTER 11

The next morning, I woke bright and early, recharged after a night of socializing with my new family. There was no sign of Hermes or Constance, so I decided to head downstairs into the kitchen. Zelda had the morning off and had arranged to come over and hang out, but she wasn't due to arrive for another hour or so. I'd had a rather peculiar dream about coffee and walnut cupcakes, and a strange inspiration was moving me to try and bake something all by myself.

First of all, I checked the small pantry and cold room that branched off from the bakery kitchen. I had a vague sense of the ingredients I would need in my head. All I had to do was see what was in stock, see what was missing, and grab the items from a local shop.

I didn't know any local shops yet, but it would give me a good excuse to get a bit of exploring in before breakfast.

The pantry was pretty sparse; naturally it would be because the bakery had been closed for almost a year. It was a medium-sized room about ten feet long and three feet wide. I had a quick scout of the shelves and when I turned back around to leave something on the shelf by the door surprised me.

CAKES TO DIE FOR

Sitting there was some flour, muscovado sugar, a jar of instant coffee, and a jar of walnuts.

"What in the..." I muttered to myself, grabbing the things and taking them into the kitchen. I wondered what the odds were of me having *exactly* the things I needed. With the items set down I went over to the fridge to see what chilled ingredients I had. Again, to my surprise, I found a tub of mascarpone cheese—still in date—and eggs that didn't expire for another two weeks. I took the ingredients out and set them on the table, feeling a little confused.

"Morning," Hermes said as he came through the back door. "Doing some baking?"

"I thought I'd try; I woke up feeling inspired. The weirdest thing is that I have *exactly* all the ingredients I need; at least I think I do. Did Constance stock the kitchen overnight or something?"

"Nope, you're enjoying the benefits of being a witch in a magical bakery. You can summon a few ingredients each day with your magical power," Hermes explained. "Where do you think the ingredients for the pancakes came from yesterday?"

"Huh, I guess I just thought Zelda had a few basic items in. All I need now then is a recipe." I pulled out my phone and went to search for a recipe, then I stopped myself.

"Looks like you're finally learning," Hermes said. "You're a kitchen witch; you *are* a recipe book. You've got generations of knowledge and intuition inside of you. Just remember what Constance said and you'll be fine. Empty your mind, imagine the end result, and the rest will happen."

"I've got this," I said, sounding a little surer than yesterday.

"You do!" Hermes said in encouragement. "And if you get time to make a fish pie too it probably wouldn't hurt."

I laughed at Hermes and rolled my eyes at the suggestion. Without much more thought I grabbed an apron off the wall, turned the radio to some station that was playing calm folky music, and I started baking.

When Zelda came through the door forty-five minutes later, she found me sitting at the table in the bakery kitchen, with a book in one hand and a cup of tea in the other. On the plate in front of me were thirteen coffee and walnut cupcakes, perfectly iced and decorated.

"Woah, Zora!" Zelda said, her eyes lighting up upon seeing the cupcakes. "Did you make these?!"

"I did indeed," I said smugly, setting my book down and biting my lip. "I haven't actually tried one yet. I'm really nervous they won't taste good."

"Allow me to throw myself on that grenade," Zelda said, and grabbed one of the cupcakes off the plate. She wasn't one for delicate little bites, and she shoved the whole thing into her mouth at once. "Mmph, mmh muph!" she said, closing her eyes and giving me a thumbs-up.

"I don't think she likes them," Hermes cracked.

Seeing Zelda eat one gave me enough courage to try. I took a small testing bite and had to blink while coming to terms with the fact that it was actually pretty amazing. "I baked this..." I said in amazement. I had another bite and a golden wave of energy burst through me.

"Not bad for your first solo batch!" Zelda said, already reaching for another one. "You'll have to open up quick so you can turn this little talent of yours into gold!"

"Baking is one thing, running a business is another. Like I can magic up a few ingredients here and there apparently, but I'm going to need cash to get this place on its feet again, and I'll need at least one other person to help me run the place, right?"

Zelda nodded. "Yeah, Constance had a girl that helped run the place. She works over at the hotel now though."

"So, I need to hire someone... that involves more money! How am I supposed to even start?"

Constance suddenly floated through the floor of the kitchen. "There's five thousand dollars in the safe. I'll tell you the combination as soon as you take boards off the front of the bakery and clean up the front room a little bit."

"Five thousand dollars?!" I said in startlement.

Zelda was confused by the outburst, then put it together. "Constance is here, isn't she?" she asked while going for a third cupcake.

"Yeah, and she says if we tidy up the front of the bakery a bit, she'll tell me the combination to the safe. There's money in there to get the business back on its feet."

"We best roll our sleeves up then and get to work!" Zelda said, putting on an old-timey voice that was meant to sound like a southern farmer.

"You're wasted not being up on a stage," I said and laughed.

"Let's not start that again. Come on, I'll help you out."

AFTER ONLY AN HOUR or so of sweeping up the floors and cleaning the dusty tables, the front room already looked much better. We turned the lights on, and I headed around the front via the alleyway and pulled the old boards off the door using a hammer. Once the boards were off, I unlocked the front door and opened it to let some fresh air into the room.

"A fresh lick of paint or two on the walls and counters and this place will look just like new!" Zelda remarked. We both stood there for a moment to regard our hard work when I heard a voice behind us.

"I'll have a cronut, with some raspberry cheesecake!" came the loud voice. Turning around I saw a large heavyset woman dressed in flowing floral gowns and multicolored silks. Her neck and wrists were overflowing with rows and rows of bead necklaces. She threw her head back and laughed. "Just kidding. I know, I know, I'm terrible."

"Marjorie?" Zelda questioned. "How can I help you?"

"I was just stopping by, my dear little Zelda. I was on my way to work when I noticed the lights were back on. Are you finally emptying out and selling the property?"

"The opposite actually," I said. "We're doing the place up and reopening."

'Marjorie' tucked her chin into her neck and turned her head, her brows lifting at the same time. The entire expression suggested she was surprised by that answer and didn't quite know what to do with it.

"Forgive my manners," she said with a delayed laugh. "I'm Marjorie, Marjorie Slade. I run the bakery on Main Street, *Sweetie Pies*. We're the best in town!" Marjorie pulled a business card from somewhere on her person and extended it to me. I took the card and glanced at it out of courtesy. My fingertips hummed faintly with vibration, and I realized Marjorie here had to be a witch too. "But who are you?" she said, regarding me with a look of keen interest. "I don't recall seeing you around here before?"

"Zora, Zora Wick," I answered. "I just moved here. I'm taking over the bakery."

Marjorie's eyes grew wide at my name. She looked at Zelda and balked. "Another Wick?! My goodness, you lot really are everywhere!"

"We're taking over!" Zelda joked.

"But really, sweetie," Marjorie said to me. I wondered on what authority she thought she could call me sweetie. "It's a big undertaking running a bakery. Hard work you know. Have you ever done something like this before?"

"No," I admitted. "But I've got Zelda and Constance guiding me every step of the way."

Marjorie blinked in alarm and laughed nervously. "But Constance is dead, dear."

"Zora can see ghosts," Zelda said smugly. "She's been talking to Constance."

"My goodness!" she said, putting a hand against her chest and looking around the room. "Is she here now? Has the poor dear shed any light on what she was doing to make her heart go kaput? Probably that yoga she was always talking about. She liked to keep fit. You know, in my youth I was quite the athlete too. A track and field star."

"Turns out ghosts don't have many memories of their last twenty-four hours," I said. "But we've turned up some information recently to suggest her death wasn't everything it seemed."

Marjorie put a hand to her head and looked away. "Heavens, well it certainly sounds like you girls have got your hands full." She chuckled again, a sound that seemed more out of habit than anything else. "Anyway, I've got to get back to Compass Cove's busiest bakery! My doors are always open if you want to come down to the shop for some advice, Zena."

"Zora," I corrected. "My name is Zora. Though Zena is a pretty badass name."

The large woman stared despairingly at the shop before smiling weakly at us and turning to leave. Once she was gone Zelda let out a long sigh and sat down in a chair. "Urgh, the last thing I was expecting this morning was a run-in with Marjorie."

"Old friend?" I joked.

"Old pain in the butt. Marjorie runs that bakery over on Main Street. When Constance was alive her place was the busiest bakery in town, people much preferred her bakes; she put love and care into them. Marjorie throws too much sugar in everything, and she charges through the nose. Her bakes are double the price of Constance's, and she puts in half the amount of effort!"

"Sounds like there's some bad blood between you and this woman."

"Me specifically, no? Constance was always complaining about her though. The kitchen witches in town all get together once a month for a monthly meeting to talk business. They do product swaps, do coupons for each other's businesses, that sort of thing."

"A rising tide lifts all boats," I said.

"Exactly. Constance said Marjorie always brought a bad energy to those meetings though. Always complaining that her rent was higher, and that everyone else had a better spot than her. I think she was bitter that she wasn't number one, but hey, she is now."

"It might be worth swinging around her place to see what she's offering. Maybe we can patch things up; try and build some bridges."

Zelda scoffed. "She'll only burn them down, trust me. Coming in here right now and acting all friendly is typical Marjorie. She'll give you trouble sooner than later; you'll see."

"Warning noted," I said, heading into the kitchen and pinning

Marjorie's card up on the board. Constance floated through the back wall, returning from her daily float around the cove.

"All done?" she asked.

"For now. We just had a visit from one of your old buddies, Marjorie."

Constance closed her eyes and pretended to shiver. "What did that silk pig want this time? Came to complain that you were cleaning up too loudly?"

"The opposite actually. She said if I need any advice, I should pop around to her bakery for help."

Constance laughed sharply. "I bet. She'll probably charge you fifty dollars an hour. The only thing that woman cares about is money, mark my words! Speaking of money, let's see what you've done with the place."

We both headed back into the front of the bakery. Constance came through the door, her eyes lighting up with a sparkle as she saw the restored front room. "Oh, amazing! We're all well on our way to reopening!"

"It needs a lick of paint of course," I commented. "But it already looks much better."

"It does!" Constance agreed. "Come on then, follow me!"

Zelda and I followed Constance into the back, where she floated over to the safe. "The combination is 1952. It's the year Patrick Swayze was born."

I walked over to the safe and crouched down as I entered the combination. "There is going to be money in this safe, right? We can't exactly reopen this bakery with old photographs of Patrick Swayze."

Constance chuckled but then stopped abruptly. "Don't be silly. I moved the photos upstairs to my bedroom."

The safe opened with a 'click' and the heavy door swung open, revealing a shelf with five stacks of neatly bundled notes. "I feel like I'm in a heist movie!" I said, taking out one of the piles of money and waving it around.

Constance rolled her eyes. "There's five thousand in there. It represents my takings for the final month prior to my death.

Normally I take the cash to the bank every week, but it was a busy month, so I was a little run off my feet."

"Five thousand a month?" I said, impressed by the taking. "You were sitting on a little gold mine here, Constance!"

"Zora dear, this little bakery was very popular. We were on the list of 'Ten Things to do in Compass Cove'. We always had a constant stream of tourists coming in. To be honest with you, I don't care about the money one bit, but after I died the money I had to my name helped Celeste and Sabrina set up their businesses, so I guess money does buy some form of happiness."

"I'm going to do this," I said determinedly. "I'll get this bakery up and running again. I'll hire someone great, we'll do tons of promotion, we'll put your bakery back on the map again."

"It's yours now, dear," she said affectionately. "Oh, that reminds me; there's a little folder at the back of the safe with the deeds and titles. We'll go through it all at some point and officially transfer the business into your name. Other than that, you have everything you need now to bring this bakery back from the dead."

"That reminds me, we have this other matter to attend to." I walked over to a filing cabinet where I locked away the glass jar of powder and pulled it out. "That biker in the park gave me the name of a pharmacist named Colin on Dixon Street. He said he'd identify this for me, no questions asked. This could give us our first proper clue."

Constance raised an approving brow. "Detective Zora's already on the case I see!"

Zelda walked into the kitchen hauling a bucket of water and a sponge. She put them down, wiped a hand across the back of her head, and sat down. "Floor is all done. You could eat off that. I'm taking a break now."

"Now?" I asked. "But I'm just about to go and visit this backstreet pharmacist and get him to identify the mysterious white powder!"

"What does that have to do with me?" she asked with a look of incredulity.

"Uh you're my backup, my muscle! What if this guy is dangerous? He's got ties with bikers. He could be bad news!"

"Well, what am I supposed to do? I'm barely over five feet tall. Sometimes I literally blow over in strong winds. I'm the opposite of muscle."

"Earth to Zelda, you've got magic."

"Not since you broke my wand!"

"Oh yeah, I forgot about that."

Constance floated between us. "Borrow my old wand, Zelda; its upstairs in my room if you have to use one. Zora's right, this man could be dangerous, and she can't go in there alone; she's not got a good grasp on her magic yet."

Zelda dropped her head against the table and groaned. "You know what, I've changed my mind. I was getting on quite well in life before I became a little sister."

"Ah stop being such a spoilsport," I said, and hugged her from behind. "You'd be lost without me; I'm your world!"

"You're a world of trouble," she muttered, pushing me off her.

"So, you'll help?"

"Fine," she said, giving in. "But you're going to buy me something nice on the way back. There's a nice little sushi place on Dixon Street."

"Sushi it is then!" I cheered. "Let's go. We've got criminals to meet with! Mysteries to uncover. Cloaks, daggers… all of that!"

"I am not digging this level of pep right now," Zelda groaned, shifting to her feet.

"Ah shush, you love it really."

CHAPTER 12

"What if this guy pulls a gun on us?" Zelda asked as we walked the few blocks over to the drug store on Dixon Street. "Should we be packing heat?"

I looked at her and smirked. "Do you have 'heat?'"

"No, and I wouldn't even know where to get a gun. They make me nervous if I'm being honest."

"Something tells me this whole situation is making you nervous," I remarked. We'd barely been walking for five minutes, and that entire time Zelda had been ruminating through endless hypothetical scenarios, predicting the many ways in which this rogue pharmacist might kill us.

"I'm a very nervous person," she admitted. "My therapist says I should just embrace it and go with the flow, but that idea makes me—"

"Nervous?" I guessed.

"Yes!" Zelda said, not seeming to find the funny side in this.

"I could do with seeing a therapist. I never could afford it back in the city, but maybe if I get Constance's bakery back off the ground, who knows?" I was hopeful for a moment, but then an ugly feeling reared its face in the back of my mind. The debt I was still carrying for Tyler after he screwed me over. All the money in Constance's safe couldn't get me in the black, and I needed that money for the business anyway.

"Now you look nervous, which is making me feel more—"

"Calm down, I get it. Just take a few deep breaths. I was thinking about my financial situation. I can run halfway across the country but there's no running from the fact that my name is still on the line for a lot of money. I can't get away from that, no matter how far I go."

"A guy in my year at school emigrated to Thailand to get away from his gambling debts. I'm pretty sure he's in some crazy jungle prison now though…"

"Yeah, I'll probably pass on that idea. I've seen enough documentaries set in third world prisons to know I'd rather be anywhere else. We should focus on the task at hand."

"Keep talking; you were distracting me. It helped make me feel better," Zelda said.

"Oh really, well uh… what do you talk about with your therapist?"

She shrugged. "I don't know. Everything really. A lot of it revolves around me thinking I've missed my chance."

I laughed. "What is that supposed to mean?"

"Well, I'm like twenty-three now, and I still don't really know what I want to do. I've never had a serious relationship; everyone else my age is successful, pregnant, or married. I've wasted my youth, I've got none of those things and I kind of just wish I could hit the reset button and go back to being seven. I'd start again and make no mistakes!"

"Seven? That seems a bit extreme."

"No, that's the perfect age. That's the last time I felt like I had everything under control. Things were simple. I went to school, I aced my tests, I got stickers when I went to the dentist. I was the queen of the world."

"How the mighty have fallen," I said in jest. We both crossed the street, reaching the block the drugstore was on. "Zel, you can't spend your whole life pining for the past. Things might have seemed better back then, but nostalgia is rose-tinted. I bet when you were a kid you wanted nothing more than to grow up."

"Well yeah—" she began.

"And now you're all grown up you want to go back to being a kid. You haven't screwed up your life, you haven't missed your mark. You're still just a kid for gosh sake! I'm two years older than you and I have none of those other things either! It might seem like everyone else has things under control, but trust me, *everyone* feels this way from time to time."

Zelda turned her head and looked at me uncertainly. "Really? Everyone?"

"Yes! It's just part of being human. Sometimes your mind is a scumbag and wants to bring you down, but you know what you say?"

"What?"

"You say, 'Not today, Satan!'" I bellowed. A woman walking towards us crossed over to the other side of the street at my outburst. "Take that, little voice in the back of your head, thank it for its *oh-so-helpful* input and tell it to sit back down!"

We both walked a few paces before Zelda said anything. "Somehow that is strangely helpful."

"Really?" I asked.

"Yeah, I mean I still don't feel great, but I think it helped a little. It helps to have someone to talk to, someone that has it all together."

"Ha!" I laughed, loudly.

"What's funny?" she asked.

"Zelda dear, I am a carnival ride held together with duct tape and popsicle sticks. One of these days something will snap and a small family from Tuscan will get launched thirty feet into the sky."

"I'm not sure if that was a confusing metaphor of if you know something ominous about carnival rides."

"Uh it's an open secret, Zel; don't go on carnival rides. This first session of big sister therapy is free, you're welcome. Please keep going to your regular therapist though. Truth told I'm probably doing more damage than good."

"No, this is good," she reflected. "I'll have loads to say about you next time I go anyway. I've got to get that off my chest."

"Me? You're going to talk about me?"

"Of course I'm going to talk about you. I found out I have a big sister this week. You don't think I'm going to bring that up?"

"That's a fair point. Oh, head's up, we're here."

We both stopped outside the drugstore and looked up at the flashing neon sign. Maybe it's because this place was recommended to me by an outlaw biker, but the entire walk over here I'd been imagining some dark back-alley room with no windows, with some big heavy guy guarding a corrugated metal door.

In reality we were standing outside a very normal looking drugstore, with a large glass window and a brightly lit interior.

"Here goes nothing," Zelda gulped.

"You're still nervous? This place looks nothing like I imagined!"

Zelda gave me a dubious look. "I know what the drugstore looks like; I've lived in this town my whole life. It's the concept of dealing with an underworld pharmacist that rattles me!"

"Let's just head inside."

We went inside the drugstore, the door playing a little electronic bell sound as it closed behind us. Currently there were no customers in the store, and I could see no one behind the counter either. Quiet elevator music floated over the aisles from speakers on the ceiling.

"We should leave while we still have the chance!" Zelda whispered to me.

"Take a deep breath and count to fifty," I said. Normally you would suggest counting to ten, but I could sense she needed extra time. "Everything is fine." I walked up to the counter and rang the bell. A few moments later a spectacled man with a buzzcut appeared through a door. He was wearing a long white lab coat.

"Afternoon!" he said heartily. "How can I help you?"

"I'm here to see Colin," I said carefully. "A friend of his recommended his services."

The man's face knit with bemused confusion. "I'm Colin. What is it you're looking for? Are you picking up a prescription, is this—" He lowered his voice and leaned in a little closer. "Is this about birth control?"

"What? No!" I said, wondering why that was his first assumption.

Colin put his hands up in apology. "I meant nothing by it. Normally when a young woman comes in and she's uneasy it's to do with *that*. My colleague Janet will be in tomorrow if you'd rather speak with another woman."

"It's not about birth control," I repeated. "Hudson sent me here. He said you could help identify something for me."

"Ah," Colin said, the sound long and drawn out with realization. "I see, well why didn't you just say that?"

"I'm not a criminal. Under the counter arrangements like this are a little bit intimidating," I explained.

Colin's response to that was completely unexpected. He laughed and pushed his glasses up the bridge of his nose. "Forgive me, I have to ask, but what exactly is it you think I do here?"

"I don't know; you work with biker gangs or something. Let's just cut to the chase. How much for you to test a powder for me?"

"Free," Colin said.

"I don't understand."

Colin reached under the counter, pulled out a pamphlet, and pushed it towards me. "Free. This drugstore is part of the Safer Streets Initiative. We test samples of street drugs for free to make sure they haven't been cut with life-threatening substances. Let's be frank; illegal drugs aren't going away anytime soon, but maybe we can save a life or two and help protect those that are caught in the throes of addiction."

Zelda and I looked at one another in surprise. I could already tell she was a little more at ease. "So, your hot biker friend wasn't recommending some backstreet pharmacist," she laughed. "He sent you to a legitimate place."

"It would seem so," I said, laughing as I also came to that realization. I looked at Colin. "Hudson comes in here?"

"The big biker guy? Oh yes, all the time. The initiative is an amnesty program, so there's no lawful repercussion. We hold and destroy all samples after testing."

"But he's a drug dealer," I said.

Colin shrugged. "I'm a pharmacist. Not a cop. Your biker friend comes in here way more than any other criminal I've ever met. He seems very concerned with the safety of his customers' well-being."

"You hear that, Zora?" Zelda asked. "He's a drug dealer *and* he's got a heart of gold. You're onto a winner!"

"Oh shush," I said, shooting her a look. "So, Colin, can you test something for us?"

"Sure, can do. What are we talking here?"

I pulled the small glass pot out of my handbag and passed it to the pharmacist. "This was found under one of the counters in my aunt's bakery. She passed a year ago, and we have reason to believe this might have something to do with her death."

Colin held the jar up to the light and turned it over, watching as the trace amount of white powder within tumbled around. "How did she die? Massive heart attack?"

"Now how on earth could you have known that?" I asked in astonishment.

"This is fentanyl," Colin said and put the jar down on the counter. "It's an extremely potent opioid used for extreme pain medication. A milligram of this can drop an athlete in peak human condition. An overdose typically leads to hypoxia, a stroke, massive cardiac arrest. If your aunt accidentally ingested some of this, she would almost certainly die."

"How can you be so sure it's fentanyl?" Zelda asked. "Don't you need to test it?"

"Oh, I'll test it to be sure, but I don't really need to. I recognize this jar. It's a glass sample jar that we use at the hospital pharmacy; I work there on Mondays and Fridays. Some fentanyl was stolen from the hospital stores last year, it caused quite a stir. There was a lot of paperwork to fill out after it happened!"

I looked over at Zelda, my eyes widening in acknowledgment. "Zel, I think we might be onto something here."

"Yeah, I'm getting that feeling too."

CHAPTER 13

"I don't think we can leave the police out of this any longer," I said to Zelda. "This is serious. We've pretty much confirmed that Constance was poisoned."

"Constance?" Colin asked from his side of the counter. "She's your aunt?"

"You knew her?" I asked.

"I mean, in passing. She owned the bakery by the park, right? I went in there a few times. She had the best brownies. Now I think about it I can see the resemblance between you both. I heard she died of a heart attack. It was last year, wasn't it?"

I nodded. "If this sample is potential evidence in a crime scene, do you still have to destroy it?"

"There are caveats. This is an unusual situation because I know this is stolen, and I know where it comes from. I will have to call the police unfortunately, and if they ask who gave me this sample, I will have to tell them, even with the amnesty."

"That's fine," I said. "We're trying to find out what happened to Constance. We have nothing to hide."

Colin picked up a phone from the wall and dialed a number. After a minute of waiting, he hung up. "The line's busy, I can't get through.

If you girls leave your contact details that'll be great. Once I get through to the police, I can get them to call you. I can also do a test and double-check this is indeed fentanyl, but I'm ninety-nine percent certain already. I know this jar."

Zelda and I thanked Colin for his time, and we exited the drugstore. On the way back to the bakery we stopped for sushi at Zelda's request. I picked up the tab to thank her for the backup.

"What kind of police station doesn't answer the phone?" I asked Zelda, thinking back to Colin getting a busy tone at the drug store.

"Uh, this is Compass Cove, Zora," Zelda pointed out. "The police department here isn't exactly a swat team response. Burt is the sheriff, and his two sons are his deputies. His wife works the desk in the station!"

"So, the police department around here is literally a mom-and-pop operation?" I asked, wondering if I was hearing this right.

"Pretty much! If there's ever a reason for the whole station to head out—and that happens maybe once a decade—no one answers the phone, because there's no one there to answer it!"

"Sounds like a really slick operation."

"They're not the best," Zelda admitted.

"I wonder if something big is happening now then?" I asked. Just as I did a police car came hurtling down the street, its sirens flashing as the car skidded around a corner and disappeared out of sight. It was heading in the direction of the park.

"Guess that answers that one," Zelda said. "Maybe a teenager set fire to a tree or something."

For the next ten minutes Zelda and I talked at random as we walked back to the bakery. Upon turning onto the street that ran by the park we saw ambulances and police cars parked up outside the park perimeter. Sirens were flashing silently, and a crowd had gathered to spectate.

"Looks like something a little more serious than a bit of arson. Let's check it out!" I shouted. The pair of us ran to the edge of the crowd trying to peer past the cordoned off park. On the other side of the police tape, I saw the four bikes parked up in their usual spot.

Paramedics had just lifted a man onto a stretcher and wheeled him into the back of an ambulance. I recognized him at once, it was the jerk from Celeste's café.

"It's the creep!" I whispered to Zelda. "They're putting him in the back of an ambulance!"

"Don't look now," Zelda said, nudging my arm. She pointed over to the right. "Looks like the police have taken an interest in your lover boy."

I looked over in the direction and saw Hudson being put into a pair of handcuffs. He didn't resist, he didn't fight. He climbed into the back of the squad car calmly, though I was sure he could have easily put up one hell of a fight.

"Zelda, Zora!" Sabrina called, running towards us as she saw us in the crowd. "Are you guys seeing this, it's wild!"

"What's going on?" Zelda asked. "We saw them put a guy into the back of an ambulance. That's the same guy that was giving Celeste a hard time yesterday!"

Sabrina's eyes were bright with energy. "I was walking through the park to come and visit you guys at the bakery when everything kicked off. Two of those bikers were having an argument and then a couple of minutes later one of them dropped to the ground. I used a little spell to eavesdrop on the paramedics from over here. Apparently, he had a massive heart attack and died. They tried to resuscitate him, but he's gone!"

I couldn't believe what I was hearing. I'd seen the jerk wad biker just yesterday and now he was dead? I looked at Zelda questioningly. "Are you thinking what I'm thinking?"

What I was thinking was this guy was in with a bad crowd, that there could be any number of reasons for his heart to fail given that he was a drug dealer. He had chosen a high stress 'career', the threat of getting thrown into jail would give me palpitations too. Maybe he had sampled the product… but you're not supposed to get high on your own supply, right?

"That there's no way a guy that young should have a massive heart attack, even if he is a total creep? You think this could be—"

"Fentanyl again? Yeah, that's exactly what I'm thinking." I looked over at Sabrina. "What's happening with Hudson? Why is he under arrest?"

"The one in the car is Hudson? The same one you're all starry-eyed for?" she asked, then added, "Wait, what's Fentanyl?"

"I'll tell you in a second. Did you hear them say why he's under arrest?"

"I couldn't eavesdrop them as well from where I was standing, but he was the one arguing with the guy that died. They've arrested him on suspicion of murder."

"Wait a second, you're saying Hudson killed that guy?" I asked in astonishment.

Sabrina looked at me and shrugged her shoulders. "Call off the wedding I guess?"

I rolled my eyes at her. "That's not what I'm thinking. I'm thinking this is all remarkably similar to Constance's death. What if Hudson killed her too?"

* * *

AFTER THE SCENE at the park, we headed back to the bakery and tried to digest the strange series of events over a cup of tea. Celeste was working at the café, so it was just Sabrina, Zelda, and me.

"I mean what are the odds," Sabrina said after we caught her up with our discoveries. "It looks like Mom was poisoned with fentanyl and died of a heart attack, and on your way back from finding that out this other guy dies of a heart attack too?"

"Very suspicious," Zelda commented.

"I know these bikers are connected somehow," I said. "If only we could jog Constance's memory a little."

"Jog my memory about what?" Constance said as she floated through the wall. As the others couldn't see her, I let them know she had arrived.

"Where have you been?" Sabrina asked, staring in the wrong direction. "We've been looking for you!"

"I was watching that spectacle outside, didn't you see?! One of those biker jerks has bit the dust!" I relayed her answer to Zelda and Sabrina before I replied, keen to avoid another game of ghostly telephone.

"We saw, we were watching in the crowd," I said. "I didn't see you anywhere. Where were you?"

Constance floated on over and set herself down on the kitchen table. "Sometimes I like to watch these events unfold from above. The world is so much different with a bird's eye view. I can move around and get all these interesting perspectives, like I'm filming a documentary! Ooh, tell Sabrina I like her dress!"

"Constance said she likes your dress," I said, relaying yet another message from my ghostly aunt.

"That means she hates it," Sabrina replied, still staring in the wrong direction as she tried to single out her mother's ghost. "What's wrong with it?!"

"It's too low-cut," Constance said. "If she wants to find a good man, she has to leave a *little* to the imagination."

"Constance said she genuinely loves it. She's turned over a new leaf since passing."

"Oh, thanks, Mom!" Sabrina said cheerily, directing her compliment to a toaster.

"Look, not that I don't love being your sole communicator to the living side," I said to Constance, "but is there really no other way for you to talk to people? Am I doomed to translate your wit for the rest of my life? "

"It's not that bad, is it?" Constance asked.

"It's getting a bit old having to repeat everything you say. I'm not a parrot."

"Squawk! I'm not a parrot!" Hermes said as he ran into the kitchen and hopped onto a chair. He chuckled to himself for a second. "What are we talking about here?"

"Zora's tired of translating for Constance," Zelda said.

"I didn't say tired, I just want to know if there's a way everyone can see and hear her." I looked at Constance, Sabrina, and Zelda in turn, hoping one of them might have an answer, but a sea of blank faces stared back at me.

"Just get used to it, Zora darling," Constance said.

"If there is, I don't know about it," Zelda added.

"Yeah, ghost sight is a rare thing, it can't be bottled," Sabrina chimed in.

Hermes just threw his head back and laughed slowly, like a villain in some camp action movie. I looked at him questioningly. "Something amused you, Hermes?" I asked.

"Yes. Don't send a witch to do a familiar's job."

"Meaning what exactly?" Zelda asked.

"Meaning you girls couldn't find a rabbit if the hat was on your head! There's a way we can make Constance more visible, but she might not like it."

"I don't like this already," Constance said in wary anticipation.

"What is it?" Sabrina asked.

"We'd have to complete a summoning circle. We each take one of Constance's most personal items and burn it while I read an incantation. After that she should be visible to each person that took an item. It will only work if the deceased had a close relationship with the person in their living life."

"No one is burning my things!" Constance said, jumping up from the table, one hand held defiantly in the air.

"How does Mom feel about that idea?" Sabrina asked, still staring in the wrong direction as she looked for her mom.

"I think she's down for it." I had to think fast as Constance hurled a salt grinder my way. I stuck my hand up at the last second and caught it.

"Me thinks Zora might be twisting the truth a little," Zelda remarked.

"Okay, she's not totally down," I admitted. "But Constance, think about it. You'd be able to talk to your daughters again. This is the chance to get back a little bit of your life." Same for me too.

"I..." she began, but she stopped just as quickly. "I'll think about it. But no one does anything until I say so!"

"She said she'll think about it," I said, placing the saltshaker on the kitchen table. I looked over at my ghostly aunt. "Hey, we've got some good news and bad news."

"Good news first," she said, floating back down to the table.

"Good news, you were right."

"Okay..." she said slowly.

"Bad news, you were right. Someone *did* poison you, with fentanyl, some super-deadly painkiller. A pharmacist identified it for us. He also said some was taken from the hospital pharmacy just over a year ago."

"By whom?!" she said animatedly.

"We don't know yet, but hey, that's a lead. We want to talk to the police about it, but they're busy with this biker that just dropped dead in the park." I sighed, wondering still why I felt there was a connection between the bikers and Constance's death. "I wish the last twenty-four hours of your life weren't such a hazy memory for you," I said. "It would be really handy if we had a clearer picture."

"Another argument for the summoning circle," Hermes piped up.

"Why's that?" I asked.

"The more people that can see Constance, the more she'll be able to remember of her last twenty-four hours. Ghosts can hardly ever remember their last day on earth, no one really knows why, but there's a way to strengthen those vague memories."

"Well, aren't you a fountain of knowledge today, Hermes?" Sabrina commented.

"The familiar job description is a simple one. Study magic and be sarcastic." Hermes began licking the back of his paw and cleaning his ears.

"You've always had the second one down, nice to see you finally practicing the first," Zelda said. Sabrina and I both laughed and let out a long 'Ooooh', to stir the pot.

"What do you say, Constance? One more reason to do this spell?"

Constance sank at the thought of her personal things being burned, but from her demeanor I could see she was definitely closer to considering it. "Not my Donny Osmond posters, they're my most valued items!"

"Hermes, can it be any old thing in particular, or prized belongings?"

"Mundane items aren't going to achieve anything. We need platinum status possessions!" Constance wailed and dropped her head to the table. I just found myself chuckling at the oddness of this all.

"What's funny?" Sabrina asked. "What's Mom doing?"

"I think she's coming to terms with the idea of seeing Donny Osmond on fire. When should we do the ritual? Tonight?"

Zelda and Sabrina both nodded their approval. "I'll message Celeste and let her know. Tonight we burn Donny."

CHAPTER 14

*L*ater that night Constance unlocked her bedroom door and granted Zelda and I brief access to retrieve three of her Donny Osmond posters, which were apparently her most treasured items in the world—I didn't quite understand it myself.

The posters were framed, and she had placed them on the floor at the foot of her bed. As I stepped into her bedroom for the first time, I found myself a little overwhelmed from the hundreds of framed pictures staring back at me from the walls and ceiling, a mixture of Donny Osmond and Patrick Swayze posters. There wasn't an empty bit of wall or ceiling to be found.

"This is uh... cute," I said as we stepped into the room.

"Yes, very relaxing," Zelda said, staring at me with wide eyes that said *are you seeing this insanity?*

"I picked three off the wall, but I can't bring myself to get them out of the door. Just hurry up and get them out before I have a breakdown!" Constance said, throwing one hand against her head like a damsel in distress.

We hurried the pictures out of the room, Constance slamming and locking the door behind us. The ceremony was taking place in the back alley behind the bakery. I'd almost burned the bakery down once since coming to Compass Cove, I wasn't going to repeat that anytime soon.

It was dark outside now and Celeste, Hermes, and Sabrina were waiting for us in the back alley, four mugs of hot chocolate waiting on an old wooden crate next to them. We joined them around the burning metal barrel, took the posters out of their frames and shared them out between Zelda, Celeste, and Sabrina. I obviously didn't need to take part in the ceremony because I could already see Constance—Hermes too.

"What's Mom's room like?" Celeste asked. "She never let anyone in there before now."

"It's uh… *different*," I said, sure I was going to have nightmares about those posters tonight. How Constance slept with so many faces staring back at her in the dark I'll never know. "Let's just get this over with and set fire to this wide-mouthed seventies idol."

"Amen to that," Celeste said. "So, this well help us all see mom's ghost?" she asked Hermes. Hermes currently sat on a dumpster, overlooking the flaming metal barrel we were using as the firepit.

"Not just that, but it might help resurface some memories from Constance's final hours," Hermes said. There was a large book open before him on the crate, its yellowed pages filled with mysterious glowing runes. I'd tried to get a closer look a few times, but he'd batted away my hand, saying I wasn't *'ready for this stuff yet!'*

"I'm confused. I thought Zora's biker boyfriend was the one that killed Mom. Didn't they just arrest him?" Celeste asked.

"They did, for murdering that other guy," Sabrina corrected. "If we can jog Mom's memory with this ritual then maybe we can find more proof to nail Zora's prison husband for that too."

I simply stared at my younger cousins, my mouth hanging open slightly. "You make the mistake of saying you find a guy attractive once… shall we continue?"

"Yes," Hermes said. "Let's. Fear Factor is on in twenty minutes, and I don't want to miss it."

"You know it's a rerun," Zelda pointed out. "You're not exactly missing cutting-edge TV. That show is like twenty years old."

"Wait, what?" Hermes said in genuine alarm. "I guess that makes sense. I thought everything looked a bit early 2000s."

"Your perception of time is somewhat a little baffling," Sabrina remarked.

"Give me a break; I'm over seven hundred years old. After a while one century blurs into another, and you humans have really started shifting gears with these stupid cultural trends. Every ten years everyone changes their hair and clothes and I'm supposed to keep up!"

"Ahem," I said, clearing my throat loudly. "Let's get on with the ritual."

"Right, right," Hermes said, refocusing himself again. "Everyone get your items ready while I prepare the incantation." Sabrina, Celeste, and Zelda all clutched their rolled-up posters in their hands and held them up triumphantly. Hermes started reading from the spell book before him. I wasn't actually sure what language he was speaking; it sounded like a mixture of Latin, Sanskrit, and straight up gibberish.

As he spoke the mysterious looking runes and symbols on the pages started to glow at random, and then a wind rose up from the ground, rushing around the space in a building cyclone.

"Commit the items to the fire!" Hermes shouted over the wind. The three of them threw their posters onto the flame. The orange flame suddenly turned green and tall, spiraling up towards the night sky as a neon funnel of curious magic. *"Oh, great specter that does roam, come forth, let yourself be known!"*

With those words the wind immediately vanished, and the fire dropped back to its normal flickering.

"I can't believe you actually did it," a voice came from behind us. I turned around and so did everyone else. There I saw Constance floating up in the air, having come out of the apartment wall.

"Mom!" Sabrina and Celeste shouted in unison. "We can see you!"

Whatever devastation Constance felt for her posters was short-lived. As her daughter's noticed her, Constance's entire demeanor changed and she rushed towards them both, and in her best effort attempted some sort of ghostly hug.

With the ritual done we went back inside, where Zelda, Celeste, and Sabrina spent a big chunk of time finally talking to each other without having to use me as an intermediary. I must admit I myself got tangled up in the talk, and it was only when Hermes wandered in an hour later that we actually got around to the crux of the matter.

"Sorry," he yawned while coming into the apartment. Sabrina was busy telling a story, but Hermes steamrolled right in and started talking over the top of her like it didn't matter. I got the impression the cat didn't care so much about social etiquette after living for so long, but cats are inherently selfish, so I guess a talking cat isn't much different. "I fell asleep by the barrel fire. It was sure toasty out there. So, any luck with the memory recall?" he posited, jumping up onto one of the remaining chairs at the table.

We all took a second and looked at one another with a collective expression that said *oh yeah!*

"Darn. We got caught up in the act of catching up," Celeste said. "Mom?"

Everyone turned their attention to Constance, who had one hand against her head in thought. "You know what, I think there actually is something else!" she said, closing her eyes while trying to recollect.

"What is it?" I asked, sitting forward on my chair.

"I was packing up the bakery for the night, when someone came around, someone unexpected—"

"Who?" Sabrina pressed.

Constance strained as she tried to dive deeper into her memory. "Argh, it's so close but so far away. It's like there are parts just missing."

"What about the park?" I said. "You mentioned you have a memory of the park at night."

"Wait, I do!" she said in alarm, opening her eyes and looking at me. "It was those darn bikers—"

"They did it?!" Celeste and Sabrina asked in unison.

"Not that," Constance dismissed. "I went to confront them in the park. I remember one of my last customers of the day, a young woman who was doing a bakery tour of the northeast. She was a little shaken when she arrived in the bakery. I asked her what was wrong, and she said those bikers in the park had catcalled her. Well after I closed up the shop I marched over there and gave them a piece of my mind."

"Mom!" Celeste reprimanded. "That is so dangerous!"

"Kind of badass though too," Sabrina pointed out.

"What did they do?" I asked. "Did they attack you?"

"No, they just laughed it off like it was some big game. I stormed back to the bakery and finished cleaning the kitchen."

"Is there any chance they could have slipped something to you? Did they follow you back to the bakery?" I asked, so far on the edge of my seat now I thought I might fall off.

"I… I can't remember!" Constance said, dropping her head against her hand. "Urgh, something's there in my head, a shape I can't see. Someone came to the bakery, but I don't know who. I feel like it was someone familiar."

"Familiar like those bikers?" Sabrina asked.

"I… I don't know," Constance sighed. "I'm sorry, girls, I really am. I'm trying my hardest here. This stuff is hard."

"If you ask me, it only established what we already suspected," Celeste said. "Those bikers had something to do with this. I just know it; I can feel it in my angry little fists. What do you think, Zora? What do we do?"

Everyone sitting at the table looked at me in expectation, and I found myself a little surprised, wondering how I'd ended up as the lead cheerleader in this amateur investigation.

"Let's call the cops." I jumped up from the table and made my way over to the flamingo phone before anyone at the table could respond. I picked up the receiver—a bright pink flamingo head—and called 911.

"Compass Cove Police Station, how may I help you?!" a chipper voice answered.

"My name is Zora Wick," I began quickly. "I have reason to believe my aunt was—"

"That's what I might say if anyone was here, but we're not!" the voice

interrupted. *"We're now closed, but please leave a message if its urgent. Feel free to call again in the morning!"*

I stared at the flamingo head for a moment before putting it back in its cradle. Upon my return to the table Zelda spoke up. "Answer phone?"

"How is this police station allowed to run?" I asked. "Crime doesn't have a closing time!"

"Uh, it does in this town," Sabrina said. "Nothing bad happens here ever; that's why the police are so lax."

"But something bad has happened, *twice!*" I pointed out.

"What do we now then?" Celeste asked me.

"I've not got a lot of ideas, but I think tomorrow first thing I'm going down to that police station to report what we've found out so far. Two healthy people have died now. If this Hudson guy is responsible, then I don't have good faith he'll stay inside. He's avoided capture so far, and I think he'll do it again."

"Wait," Zelda said. "Do you think he could come after us? He knows you're looking into this thing! Maybe he bumped off his friend because he was going to say something!"

The realization hadn't dawned on me so far, but as soon as Zelda sowed that seed, I could see everyone at the table suddenly grow a little more concerned.

"I wasn't thinking that, but I sure as heck am now," Sabrina muttered gravely.

"One thing's for sure," I said. "I'm going to speak to the police, and I'm going to get answers."

CHAPTER 15

"Sorry I can't give you answers, this is an ongoing investigation, and all parties are entitled to their privacy. Have a good day!" The woman on the other end of the line hung up before I could get another word in.

"Let me guess," Hermes said. "That call didn't go quite exactly as you planned."

It was the following morning and, to my surprise, I actually managed to get through to the police station. The chipper woman that answered the call shut my line of inquiry down very quickly though. She hadn't even given me a chance to bring up the fact that I suspected Constance's death was due to murder.

"I'm going down there," I growled, putting the flamingo phone back down and marching over to the kitchen table to finish my coffee.

"Is that wise?" Hermes asked. "I mean, you just moved here. The last thing we want is you getting arrested for assaulting a police officer."

"Who said anything about assault?!" I choked, almost spitting out my drink.

"No offense, Zora, but you give me that kind of vibe. You're that crazy chick who snaps out of the blue."

"I have never snapped and will never snap. I'm just trying to get answers; I'm not some high-strung psycho."

"If you say so," Hermes said, rolling his eyes for good measure before hopping down from his chair. "I'd ask if you want an accomplice, but I've got a very important nap scheduled, so my paws are pretty full."

"Your absence will be greatly felt," I replied. "How on earth am I going to find out what happened to Constance without a wisecracking cat at my side?"

"Hey, I'm the one that pulled through with that ritual last night. As far as I see it, old Hermes deserves a little thanks," he said, hopping onto the cushioned bench that ran along the apartment windows.

"Ah, you're right," I said with a note of defeat. "Still, we're a long way from discovering what happened to Constance. I better get ready and go down to the station. We need answers. Fast."

I headed back to the spare bedroom—which I guess was just my bedroom now—changed out of my pajamas and into a dress, tights, jacket, and boots. Hermes was already asleep when I walked back into the lounge, so I locked up and walked into town, heading in the direction of the police station.

I'd made it about one block when Constance's ghost came floating out of the pavement, right through the middle of a passing man who obviously couldn't see her.

"Sweet mother of mongoose!" I hissed, almost jumping out of my skin. "Can't you just appear like a normal person?"

"Sorry," she said, falling in line and floating beside me while I continued to walk down Main Street. "I was exploring down in the sewers. There's lots of weird things down there. If anything, that's the one upside of being a ghost; you get to go anywhere you like."

"Well, that does sound pretty cool. Is there a limit on how far you can go?"

Constance shook her head. "If there is I haven't found it yet. Obviously, I can only float so fast, not much quicker than regular running speed. I can't exactly get on public transport, so there are limits to how far I can travel. I went down to Manhattan a few weeks after I died; that took me about a month. I figured I could watch every single Broadway show for free while I was there. I was singing musical numbers all day long! I spent another month exploring the city, and then I came back again."

"Why? I bet you could spend forever exploring that city and never run out of things to do."

"I'd definitely go back, but a part of me felt like I should come home again and be close to Sabrina, Celeste, and Zelda. Ever since I passed, I've spent a good amount of time just watching them and making sure they're okay. I don't want to miss out on their lives."

"Hey, be careful, that almost sounded sentimental," I joked.

"I'm on my way to visit Celeste actually. I already stopped in to see Sabrina this morning. I must say I'm still rather devastated I had to lose those posters of Donny but being able to drop in and talk with my daughters is amazing. I almost feel like I'm alive again. Where are you headed?"

"Down to the police station. I want to tell them you were poisoned. We need to throw everything we can at this Hudson guy. I'll have to—" I paused, seeing a bakery on the other side of the street. A large sign over the window said '*Sweetie Pies*'. "Wait, is that Marjorie's bakery?"

"Uh, don't get me started on Marjorie," Constance said derisively. "Make sure you've had your morning cup of coffee before dealing with her."

"She's not that bad, is she?" I asked. "She popped into the bakery the other day to offer her support. Maybe I should swing by quickly and show my face. I need to start making allies in this town, especially if I want to get the bakery up and running as quickly as possible."

"I'm taking that as my cue to leave then," Constance said. "I'll see you later. Good luck with Marjorie!" Constance floated off through the corner windows of a clothing shop and disappeared out of sight.

I waited for a car to pass and skipped across the road to Marjorie's bakery. As I walked through the door a little bell chimed overhead. It was early in the morning still, so there weren't any other people inside the bakery at the moment. The first thing to catch my attention was an amazing chocolate sculpture set upon the counter. If this is what I was competing with, I wasn't sure I could keep up.

On a wall to my right there was a display cabinet filled with pictures, trophies, and medals of what looked to be a young Marjorie in track gear. I recalled her saying she had been a track and field star, and from this small shrine she was obviously proud of her past.

I approached a young woman running around quickly behind the counter. She was pale, short, and thin, with dark hair and glasses that almost looked as strong as mine.

"Good morning, I won't be a minute!" she said hastily, twirling around on the spot and dashing all over as she quickly filled up the glass display cabinets. My fingertips vibrated ever so slightly, and the girl looked up at me. "Oh, thank goodness, you're a witch."

With a snap of her fingers, cakes and pastries started flying off trays and lining themselves up neatly in the display cabinets.

"I can come back if you're busy?" I asked.

"No, it's fine; I'm just running the back *and* the front this morning, things are a little—" Beeping suddenly came through a door on the rear wall and the girl's eyes opened wide. "Ah! The cheesecake! Be right back!"

She dashed out of the room, leaving me alone in the front of the bakery. I looked over the selection of items in the glass display cabinets. Everything looked very nice, certainly visually pleasing enough to do well on social media. People are always posting pictures of cakes and pretty pasties.

A moment later the girl darted back out again, addressing me with a customer-facing smile. "Alrighty, how can I help you this morning?"

"My name is Zora Wick. I actually stopped by to see Marjorie. I just inherited Constance's old bakery by the park."

"Ooh, Constance's place is reopening? That's exciting! I'm Daphne," Daphne said, holding out her hand. We shook. "Marjorie's upstairs sorting out some paperwork; she's a little run off her feet with the business side of things this morning. Would you like me to pass on a message?"

"No, I'm just a friendly neighbor popping in to say hello. I can always drop by again tomorrow." I paused and looked around, my attention settling on the pictures and trophies celebrating Marjorie's sporting achievements.

"Hard to believe, eh?" Daphne said. "But she can still run with the best of them, even considering her... you know—" Daphne gestured to indicate Marjorie's larger size. "That woman is surprisingly fast when she wants to be."

"It seems like Marjorie has more than a few surprises up her sleeve! Say, while I'm here I might as well try out the merchandise." I said, my eyes poring over the offerings. My eyes came back to the sculpture of the chocolate swan again. "Say, this is pretty breathtaking; who did this?"

"That's Marjorie. Sculpture is her real forte," Daphne said. "She doesn't give much credence to her abilities, but that woman can turn a hunk of chocolate into the most amazing artwork."

"How do you even do that?" I said as I marveled the sculpture. "I wouldn't even know where to begin."

"Oh, patience, and lots of freeze spray! The sculpture is already accounted for unfortunately though. It's going to a corporate event later today. You can pick anything from the display cabinets though," Daphne said, gesturing to the offerings under the brightly lit glass.

"Did you bake all of this?"

"I... did, following Marjorie's in-house recipes!" she said, her smile wavering a little.

"You seem unsettled by that!" I commented.

"No, no, everything is fine. I mean I tend to work without recipes, that's just my brand of kitchen witch. Marjorie has her own way and that's great too. This is her shop, so I follow her rules."

"Right... well what would you recommend?"

"The uh..." Daphne said, also scanning the contents while she tried to settle on one. Something told me that if Daphne didn't work here, she wouldn't recommend anything, but being an employee she obviously couldn't say that. "Well, if you like sugar anything here will hit the spot. Marjorie likes her recipes sweet!"

"What's the least sweet thing?" I asked.

"Probably the bran muffins, but even they—" She stopped herself. "They're a great way to start the morning!" Stellar sales pitch.

"Sounds great, ring me up one of them." Daphne did so and I paid up. I was about to say goodbye and leave when Marjorie came through the door behind the counter. She looked tired and her eyes were red as though she had been crying.

"Wick," she said with a note of surprise. "I was just looking at the cameras. I thought that was you. You're not swinging by to steal ideas, are you?" Marjorie asked. She framed the question as a joke, but there was an edge to her voice that made me suspect she had genuine concerns.

"You know what they say about imitation!" I joked back. "I was actually just stopping by to show my face and say hello. You know, being neighborly and all that."

"Well, isn't that splendid of you," Marjorie said with a slight smile. "You'll have to forgive me; I'm not feeling too great today—"

"The paperwork," Daphne said quickly. "I already told Zora you're tied up with paperwork."

Marjorie glared at Daphne disapprovingly. "Yes... that as well. It's one of those days. You'll have to excuse me, Zora, but I must get back to it. Lots to take care of. You'll learn this, running a business isn't all cakes and cookies," Marjorie said in a rather condescending way.

"Thanks for the heads-up. I was going to sign the business deeds in chocolate sauce!" I joked back. Marjorie didn't seem to approve of the joke. "Is everything okay?" I added quickly, noting her red eyes. "You look like you've been crying."

"Crying is for the weak, Wick. I've only cried once in my life, and that was the day I watched ET at the local cinema as a child."

"Ah yes," I recollected. "The bit where he leaves at the end? Very sad."

"What? No! The fact that the incompetent military types let that disgusting little rat-faced freak escape and live! I was devastated!" Marjorie snapped.

"Right," I said after a long pause, sharing a silent side glance with

Daphne, who was now staring down at the floor. "Well, I'm going to skedaddle, lots to see, lots to do. Have a good day now!"

"I always do," Marjorie said. As I turned to run out the door the sight of a huge inanimate golden retriever scared the life out of me. I'd somehow failed to notice the giant charity box dog when I walked into the café. I sidestepped the monstrosity and quickly scuttled out of the shop before embarrassing myself any further.

"Yikes," I muttered to myself when back on the street. That woman had a way of making a room feel tense, I was starting to understand what Constance and Zelda meant.

I decided to give Marjorie the benefit of the doubt. It *did* look like she had been crying, so maybe she had some heavy stuff going on in her personal life that she didn't want to talk about. I know when my dad died, I wasn't myself for quite a while. I was a little more detached than usual, and colder with people too.

I hadn't walked out of that situation empty-handed though and unwrapped the pleasant looking bran muffin and took a bite while I carried on down the street to the police station. I ran straight over to the nearest trash can and spat the muffin out, throwing the rest of it in too. A man was sitting on a bench next to the trash can while he waited for the bus. He stared at me in bewilderment for a second.

"That is way too much sugar!" I shouted, feeling a need to justify how crazy I looked right now. The man looked away slowly, turning his attention back to his newspaper. I quickly hurried away from the trash can, not wanting to establish a reputation already as the local crazy woman that shouted at people.

Holy heck, that cake was too sweet. If I didn't know any better, I'd say that thing was almost ninety percent sugar. Now I know why Daphne had been hesitant to recommend anything. If that was the least sweet thing on the menu, I dreaded to think what the rest of the offerings were like. Marjorie's tastebuds had to be fried from decades of sugar-abuse, because there was no way a normal person could think that tasted good.

"Note to self, never order anything from Marjorie's bakery again if you want to keep your teeth," I said to myself quietly, still hurrying in

CAKES TO DIE FOR

the direction of the police station. The bran muffin had only been in my mouth for a second, and it still felt like my mouth was covered in a fuzzy layer of sugar. My dentist was probably going to have a field day with this one.

That was another thing I had to sort out. Find a new dentist, find a new doctor. I'd only been here for a few days, and during that entire time I'd been busy handling this trouble with Constance and the bakery. I had to return the rental car too, but I had until the end of the week to do that at least.

Ten minutes later I arrived at the police station, which was about three-quarters down along Compass Cove's Main Street, heading in the west direction. I did think about driving to make the trip a little shorter, but I'd always liked walking and I wanted to take in as much of the town as possible. I always did that better at walking speed. I'd already spotted a boardgame shop, a nice-looking florist, and an upmarket salon—things that I likely would have missed if zooming past in a car.

Another added benefit of walking is that it always seemed to clear my mind too, and there was definitely enough going on at the moment that my mind resembled a screaming pit of baboons at feeding time in a zoo.

The police station was set back a little from the main road, with a nice bit of greenery in front of it. A tan path cut a straight line through a well-manicured lawn and bright flowerbeds. A set of automatic glass doors opened, leading into a sleepy looking police station that hadn't been redecorated since the late 80s. Sitting behind the reception desk was a large black woman in a police uniform. Her hair was a beautiful mess of thick black curls. She looked up at seeing me enter and addressed me hastily.

"Quick!" she hollered. "Six lettered word! *Amateur photographs can often be—*"

"Be what?" I asked, not understanding what was happening here.

"Well, I don't know, that's the clue for my crossword. If you want my help, then I need the answer!" she bellowed.

A bemused smile broke across my face. "I thought your job was to protect and serve. I missed the caveat about providing crossword answers in return."

"Well, I just added it, sugar, so get with it or get out of the way; now what's the answer?!"

I thought about it for a moment and then the answer came to mind. "Ah, it's quite simple when you think about it. *Blurry*. Amateur photographs can often be *blurry*."

The woman behind the counter became animated with excitement and filled it in. "That's it, it's blurry! Oh, I just knew when you walked in, and I saw those bottlecaps on your face, you'd be a crossword dork just like me!"

"Actually, I kind of hate them, but I am pretty good at them."

"Alright, sweetie pie, lay it on me," she said, putting down her crossword. "How may I help you?"

"My name is Zora Wick. I think I may have spoken with you on the phone this morning. It was concerning—"

"Right, right," she interrupted. "I remember now. You wanted to know about the fracas at the park yesterday. Well, I'm sorry, pop tart, but I'll say again what I said to you on the phone this morning, I can't go spilling the beans about ongoing investigations to just anybody, even if they *are* good at crosswords!"

"Listen, Officer—"

"Linda," she said. "Linda Combs, my husband Burt is the Sheriff, and my two sons work here too. We're a small family operation."

"Well, Linda," I said, "I think I might have information relevant to the event at the park yesterday. That biker, he died of a heart attack, right?"

Linda narrowed her eyes at me suspiciously. "Now how on earth could you know something like that, cupcake?" she said with an air of distrust. I realized that information wasn't publicly available yet, and I'd possibly revealed my hand a little too early.

"I heard it through the crowd," I sputtered quickly. "You know what gossip is like, spreads like wildfire!"

"Hmm," Linda said. "It sure does seem so. So, tell me, Zora Wick,

CAKES TO DIE FOR

what information do you have that would lend itself to yesterday's events?"

"My aunt is Constance Wick, or *was* Constance Wick—"

"Oh gosh," Linda said in a moment of recognition. "You're *a* Wick. I don't know why I didn't put it together earlier. Your family is well known around here, Zora; you're new to town though, aren't you? I haven't seen you here before."

"I guess I'm the long-lost relative. I just moved back here."

"I see. Constance's passing was just over a year ago, right? It was sad to lose her. Best bakery in town, bar none. What could the events at the park yesterday have to do with Constance?" Linda asked.

"Constance didn't just die of a heart attack. I think she was poisoned with fentanyl. We found a small pot under one of her kitchen cabinets and had it analyzed at the pharmacy."

"Hold the phone," Linda said as she leafed through scattered papers on her desk. "I do remember getting a voice message last night from the gentleman at the pharmacy. I made a note… here it is!" she said, holding up a piece of paper. "Call 'Z Wick' regarding suspected fentanyl poisoning. Well, what do you know?" Linda said in recognition and looked back at me. "You *are* on my to-do list for today."

"Look, if the guy in the park yesterday died of a heart attack, then I think he might have died of fentanyl poisoning too. I know you can't give out all the facts of an ongoing investigation, but it seems like too much of a coincidence for two healthy people to drop dead of heart attacks, especially in such close proximity to one another! I think those bikers had something to do with Constance's death—"

"Why would you think that?" Linda said, raising a brow.

"I have it on good authority that she had an altercation with those bikers the night of her death. Now you've arrested this Hudson guy and I'm guessing he's your suspect; I think he might be Constance's killer too—"

"Hold on a second, sugar bun," Linda said. "How in the holy moly do you know about Hudson?"

"Well, I was there at the park yesterday. I saw you put him in the car—"

"But how do *you* know his name?" she asked. "Are you affiliated with these bikers or something?"

"What? No!" I said in surprise. "I'm looking into Constance's death, and I talked to Hudson earlier in the week. I already said I suspected they had something to do with it, so I talked to them."

"Let me get this straight, you—a tiny, pale, petite girl—marched up to a bunch of bikers and started grilling them? You're either dumber than a turkey or you've got more balls than a caddy convention."

"Probably a little of both," I said. "I'm a journalism major; I guess I'm sort of drawn to this stuff."

"What, getting yourself into dangerous situations? Sure sounds like it. Listen, as things stand, we've not got much to go on. Besides all that, we're up to our eyeballs at the moment trying to get the roads in and out of town cleared after the landslide. Burt and the boys haven't been in the station for weeks."

"You've got Hudson in custody though, right?" I asked. "You must have had good reason to arrest him."

"I..." Linda began, but she then stopped herself. "Sorry, Zora, but I'm not allowed to talk about it. I'm allowed to say one thing though and it's this—Hudson isn't under arrest, and he isn't currently here at the station."

"Wait a second, what?!" I said in alarm. "You mean to tell me that killer is just waltzing the streets free?!"

"We had no evidence to suggest he's a killer, and his other two friends at the park claimed as much as well, though I recognize their word has to be taken with a pinch of salt."

"What about this fentanyl?" I asked. "It was stolen from the hospital pharmacy. That has to count for something. Maybe go over there, check the surveillance footage, see what you can dig up?"

"Darling, we're spread thin at the moment. If the police were butter and this town was bread, there'd be a lot of unbuttered bread. You've obviously got the credentials to snoop around and ask questions. I always wanted to be one of those investigative journalists."

"I mean I have a degree, but that's just words on paper," I said. "I'm not authorized to do anything."

"Sugar plum, this here is Compass Cove, you understand? Give a duck a clipboard and he could probably wander into a bank vault. You've already been meddling with biker gangs, and something tells me you ain't going to stop until you get answers, so I might as well help you out."

"By sending someone to look into it?" I asked, leaning over the counter to watch as Linda ducked out of view. She popped up a moment later after rummaging through a drawer; she was holding a lanyard.

"Would if I could, gumdrop, really, I would. Here, take this. You're officially Compass Cove PD's newest private investigator." Linda handed me the lanyard. I looked at it and read back the words.

"This is a lanyard for a 'Police Station Guest.'"

"Wrong, that's your express ticket behind the red tape of this town. Flash that bad boy and you'll get in anywhere," Linda said with a wink.

"I couldn't get into a public library with this thing," I replied.

"Sure, you can, and if anyone gives you a problem get them to call the station and I'll tell them different! Old Linda will scare them straight."

"What about a gun? Do I get a gun?"

Linda snorted. "You sure don't."

"Taser?" I asked.

"Do you have time to complete an intensive four-day training course?"

"So, you're sending me out there defenseless?" I asked.

"Once again, Zora, I'll remind you that you're the one going out there. I'm simply accepting the inevitable and giving you the tools you need to succeed," Linda pointed out. She looked down at her open drawer. "Ooh, I can give you pepper spray!" She threw a small black spray bottle at me, and I caught it.

"I just take the cap off and spray it?"

"Into the eyes of someone trying to harm you, yes. Don't make me regret giving you that. You know how to point and spray something, right?"

"Yes," I said slowly, opting to omit my recent run-in with a fire extinguisher.

"Well, what are you waiting for? Get out on the road, P.I Wick! Sounds like there's a juicy lead waiting for you down at that hospital!"

"I'm not really a P.I, am I?" I said. "I mean... this is just a lanyard."

"And this is just a piece of metal stuck to leather!" she said, pointing at her police badge. "People respond to authority and confidence above all. As long as you've got them, you're all good to go."

I looked down at the lanyard and pepper spray in my hands, not sure if I should feel grateful or not for this run-in with Linda. The police station wasn't able to help me look into this case, and Linda had effectively put the law in my hands, and very little in the way of tools.

"This station needs a bigger budget," I said grimly.

"Try telling that to the mayor! We've been sáying that for years! Good luck out there. You holla if you need anything. I tucked my card in that lanyard; it's got my direct line on it."

I shuffled out of the police station, wondering what had just happened here. The police weren't going to help, or weren't able at least. It really looked like this was down to me. If we wanted answers about Constance's death, I had to take charge.

Whether I wanted to or not.

CHAPTER 16

On my way back to the bakery, I had to pass Celeste's café, so I thought I'd pop in and see Celeste and Zelda as I was in the area. The café was already half full, even though it was still early morning. Celeste's ability to rustle up a nice savory breakfast was clearly appreciated by the citizens of Compass Cove.

Upon walking in, I saw Celeste and Zelda bickering about something behind the counter. There currently wasn't a queue, so I walked right up to them. "Morning," I said. "Keeping busy?"

"Trying to reason with an insane person more like," Celeste responded. "Please try and talk some sense into your little sister!"

Zelda rolled her eyes and laughed to herself.

"What's the argument this time?" I asked.

"Die Hard," Zelda said succinctly. "We're arguing about which film is the best from the series."

"How many even are there now? Like six or something?" I asked.

"Three," they both said in unison.

"I'm pretty sure there's more than three," I said. I definitely remembered watching a newer one a few years ago, though admittedly it wasn't a good as the original three.

"We're talking the original trilogy," Zelda pointed out. "Let's not kid ourselves, those three films are the best. You have to pick one of them. I said Die Hard 2 is the clear winner, but Celeste disagrees; she says the first film is the best."

"Well Celeste would be correct," I said, taking my cousin's side. "Are you out of your mind, Zelda? How is two better than one? That film is one giant plot hole from start to finish!"

"That's what I said!" Celeste said animatedly. "The planes could have just landed at another airport!"

"Um, they very explicitly state that none of the planes have enough fuel to reach another airport," Zelda explained. "They take like three seconds to cover that vital plot point."

Celeste was the one to roll her eyes this time. "That's why the first film is still the best. Nothing needs explaining, nothing needs examining. It's ninety minutes of good old-fashioned, balls-to-the-walls action. Guns, explosions, fights, just the good stuff!"

"Sorry, Zel," I said. "Looks like you're outvoted two to one here; the original wins."

"No way; this isn't over," she said. "I'm getting Sabrina's vote later. Anyway, how's your morning been?"

"Oh, not too bad. I stopped by Marjorie's bakery to say hello." Celeste and Zelda both grimaced at the same time. "Listen, I was trying to be friendly, but perhaps I should have taken heed of the warnings. Marjorie does have a way of making things tense. I feel like she doesn't trust anyone."

"She's very paranoid," Celeste recollected. "If you avoid her, she's not much of a problem, but lots of people in this town have tried doing nice things for her, and they always end up regretting it."

"I should have paid attention to Constance. I saw her on the way over there. She said she was going to swing by here and say hello."

"She already did," Celeste confirmed. "She's the one that got us on this whole Die Hard talk in the first place. You'd think now she could talk to us again she might ask how we're doing or whatever, but no, she just floated through the door and started talking about how hot Bruce Willis was in his prime. Do you know how hard it is to serve customers when there's a ghost floating over your shoulder talking at length about 'peak glutes'?"

"And we can't exactly respond," Zelda said, "because we're the only ones that can see her. The customers would think we're crazy."

"I'm pretty sure the customers already thought that; luckily you serve up good food. Where's Constance now?"

"After talking down my ear for fifteen minutes she said, 'Lovely to talk, see you later!' and then she floated off through the ceiling to go and bug Sabrina." Celeste snickered. "She's her problem now! How long did you spend at Marjorie's?"

"Oh, not long. I was mostly speaking with a girl that works there, Daphne, is it? She was a little run off her feet, covering the front and back by herself."

Celeste nodded in recognition. "Daphne is a great kitchen witch. It's a shame she's stuck working for a miserable old toad like Marjorie. I heard Marjorie makes her staff stick to very strict recipes, and we all know how much that woman loves sugar," Celeste said, addressing that last part to Zelda.

"Yeah, I tried a bran muffin. I was trying to be polite... that was a mistake. Marjorie did come downstairs; it looked like she had been crying. She's an odd one."

"Have you been to the police station yet?" Zelda asked.

"Just. I had the pleasure of meeting Linda, though she only talked to me because I successfully solved a crossword puzzle for her."

Celeste and Zelda laughed in acknowledgment. "That sounds like Linda alright," Zelda agreed. "Did you tell her everything?"

"Everything, but she wasn't much help. She said they're already spread thin enough as it is. They've not got the manpower to cover a year-old case, they're too busy trying to clear the roads. She basically gave me a lanyard, some pepper spray, and told me to go on my merry way. She wants me to look into it!"

"Glad to see my tax dollars are hard at work," Celeste said begrudgingly.

"And get this, they let that Hudson guy go! Linda said he wasn't even under arrest!"

"What?!" Celeste and Zelda said in unison, their alarm mutual.

"So, he can just waltz in here and kill us!" Celeste said in panic. Half of the customers in the café were looking at her now. She laughed awkwardly. "Uh… just rehearsing for a play, folks, back to your meals!"

"Smooth," Zelda said.

"You both need to relax, okay? Hudson doesn't even know you guys exist. If anything, I'm probably the one in trouble. It looks like the police don't have the capability to take care of this and find answers, so it's kind of down to me to look into things. I'm heading over to the hospital pharmacy now to see if Colin will let me see the surveillance footage."

"What surveillance footage?" Celeste asked.

"From the hospital pharmacy," I repeated. "Colin, the pharmacist, said some fentanyl was stolen from the hospital pharmacy just over a year ago, right before Constance died! We talked about this the other night!"

Celeste blinked as though I was explaining quantum physics to her. "I'm not really a detail orientated person, all this mystery business… it doesn't make sense to me. I'm good at the simple things, like baking delicious savory food."

"That's not simple at all," I said in her defense.

"Hey, I do know one thing about mysteries," Celeste said. "It's always the person you least suspect."

"I guess we should fly to Rome and arrest the Pope then," Zelda jibed.

Celeste rolled her head dramatically as she looked at Zelda. "Really, the Pope? A less likely person would be an astronaut on the international space station."

"I was pointing out that your rule is dumb and doesn't make any sense," Zelda said.

"I'll tell you what's dumb!" Celeste began. "Die Hard 2! How you think that's the better—"

"Okay, guys, I'm going to go now," I said loudly, keen to get out of there before their bickering resumed. "Just one girl and a can of pepper spray, going to find a killer."

"Go visit Sabrina," Celeste said.

"Why?" I asked.

"Stop by her magic shop and ask her for some defense help. If you're crossing paths with a killer, then you'll need more than pepper spray. You're a witch, Zora. You need to learn how to defend yourself with magic!"

Now *that* finally felt like a useful piece of information. "That's actually not a bad idea. Sabrina can really help with that?"

"She can get you started with some quick fixes," Zelda said. "Though really you'll have to sign up to a night class at the local college. They have catch-up courses for adult witches and wizards."

My heart lit up at the prospect. "Magic school? Are there houses? Do I get an owl? Is there a wise old man with a long silver beard? A big, enchanted castle?!"

"Replace enchanted castle with a dingy classroom in the local college and you're halfway there," Celeste said. "I taught a few classes there on a voluntary basis. It's quite fun."

I added 'Sign up to Magic School' to my mental to-do list, ignoring Celeste's realistic painting of magic education as an adult. In my head I was taking a charming steam train across the English countryside to a magical fortress full of adventure, friendship, and danger. I must have got lost in a daydream; Zelda definitely realized it.

"She's gone, away with the fairies," Zelda said to Celeste. "She's probably running around forbidden forests and fighting dark wizards."

"When do I tell her it's more like polystyrene tile ceilings and coffee-ringed tables?" Celeste whispered back.

"Eh, let her have her fun for now," Zelda said.

* * *

AFTER SNAPPING out of my daydream I headed back to Constance's bakery to get my rental car, which was parked on the street outside.

Although I preferred walking, I would have to do a little bit of driving this morning as the hospital was way over on the east side of town. After looking it up on the internet I found out that walking there and back would take an hour, so I decided the car was the best option.

It was a good choice too, because as I pulled away from the bakery it started to rain. I turned on the windshield wipers, glad I'd taken Zelda's advice to heart about always packing a raincoat around here.

After ten minutes of directions from my phone I pulled up outside Sabrina's magic shop, which was a few blocks back from Main Street. This part of town seemed a little quieter, though there were still several shops dotted between residential apartment blocks, and the sidewalks still had a generous amount of people going about their daily business.

As I climbed out of the car, I looked up at the exterior of Sabrina's magic shop, overwhelmed by feelings of mystery and enchantment. The stone-faced building was a whimsical display of gothic architecture, a looming edifice of detailed carvings that crept up four narrow stories. Four windows across on each floor, the brickwork was painted black, and the windows and trim painted purple. The place definitely looked the part. Large glass windows at the front of the shop gave a glimpse of dark and cluttered displays within and painted on the glass in extravagant looping white letters was the shop name: *Wytch's Bazaar.*

I stepped inside the shop, a tall room filled with all sorts of items, a dark wooden staircase twisting up to a mezzanine level above. Framed pictures and bookshelves filled the walls. Everywhere I looked I saw hundreds of items cluttered over dark countertops and wooden tables; every surface filled to the brim. Unusual windchimes and dreamcatchers dangled all around, mystic vines in this jungle of magical clutter.

The scent of incense filled my nostrils, and I felt a strange peace and intense curiousness to lose myself exploring the many shelves of this shop. "Hello?" a voice called from somewhere on the second floor. "I'll be down in a second!" I recognized the voice as Sabrina's.

"It's Zora!" I shouted back, walking through the shop, the fingers on my right hand trailing along the edge of a table. There were narrow walkways of space between the cluttered tables making up the shop floor. "I like your store!"

"Oh thanks, I've put a lot of work into it!" Sabrina shouted. I heard feet on the spiral staircase, and as I looked up, I saw Sabrina coming down, holding a large box of dusty leatherbound books. Her long hair was tied back with a black hairband, the sleeves of her plaid shirt rolled up to her elbows. "I've been up in the attic pulling out some old stock," she said, setting the box down and wiping her forehead. Her face was red from the effort. "Didn't expect to see you this morning. Fancy a cup of tea?"

"Go on then," I said. Sabrina motioned for me to follow her, and I did, walking behind the counter and through a door at the back of the shop that led into a charming little apartment that was just as cluttered.

"Welcome to Casa de Sabrina," she said. "Sorry for the mess. To be honest I quite like mess. It keeps me invigorated. Celeste is all about the neat and tidy… it used to drive me up the wall as a kid; we shared a bedroom growing up."

I sat down on Sabrina's couch. A few minutes later she came over with an old black kettle; she poured us two cups of tea and scratched the ears of a cat sitting next to her. Until now I hadn't noticed the cat. "Another familiar?" I asked.

"No, this is just a regular old cat. This here is Hayley. Familiars are quite rare these days, you're very lucky to have one. Mind you, Hermes is an absolute pain in the backside; I don't envy you one bit!" she laughed.

"I must admit I do feel a little self-conscious inheriting the bakery and the apartment. It was your mom's after all. I feel like some of it should have gone to you and Celeste."

Sabrina wrinkled her nose in disagreement. "Nah, it's very important for a witch to find her own way. Celeste and I never wanted the bakery. She doesn't like baking, and I'm not even a kitchen witch. Mom never inherited the bakery from her mom; she was an apprentice to another witch that used to own the place, Millicent something.

Gah, what was her last name?" She batted at the air as if giving up on remembering it.

"That makes me feel a little better, I guess. This place is really lovely by the way. I actually came here for a bit of help. Celeste said I should stop by; you might be able to help me with some defensive magic."

"Oh?" Sabrina said, setting her cup down on the table and lifting a brow in intrigue. "Are you expecting trouble?" I caught Sabrina up to speed with my morning so far, with my run-in with Marjorie, to my trip down to the police station. Upon hearing the police weren't going to help, Sabrina scoffed and rolled her eyes. "Sounds about right. Well, if they've released that murdering biker boyfriend of yours then I suppose we should give you something to defend yourself. I'm a bit limited as to what I can offer at the moment because you've not learned any proper magic yet."

"Celeste said something about a night school at the local college for adult witches and wizards?"

"That's right," Sabrina said and nodded. "You should sign up right away. I imagine you'll be caught up in no time. We'll all chip in of course, try and teach you what we can in our spare time. As things stand though you're allowed to have a wand because you're an adult. Give me a second; I think I've got just the one for you."

Sabrina hopped up from the couch and ran back through the door that led to the shop. Two minutes later she was back clutching a tall stack of long narrow black boxes. She set them down on the table and opened up the first one. Inside I saw a long dark wand, all twisted and crooked.

"This is a wand," she said, pulling it out of the box and holding it up. "It might just look like a stick—and that's because it kind of is, but it's designed to help channel magic and intention."

"Let me guess, a unicorn hair through the core?" I joked.

Sabrina laughed. "Not quite *that* theatrical. These wands are soaked in oils. This wand is rowan wood glazed with Anjelica and Feverfew. Herbs and daisies." She passed the wand over to me and I ran it through my fingers, the grain feeling pleasant against my fingertips. The wood smelled like bitter nettles.

"It's lovely," I remarked.

"No reaction though," she said, taking the wand back off me and stuffing it back into its box. "Try this one, Lemongrass and Pepper."

Following this, Sabrina and I quickly worked our way through the stack, filtering through two dozen wands in the next couple of minutes. I don't know what Sabrina was looking for exactly, but she didn't seem satisfied with any of them.

"Hm," she said after a moment of reflection. "It's strange. You're a kitchen witch, so you should have reacted with at least one of these wands... unless."

"Unless what?" I asked, wondering where she was going as she dashed out of the room again. Sabrina came back with five more boxes, looking quite excited as she quickly set them down and pulled out the first. "Okay, try this one. It's a wand for a Cosmic witch. This one has flecks of iron-nickel pushed into it, see?" she said. I took the wand and saw the flecks pushed along the ridge in a line, like a crown. "Comes from meteorite."

"Now that is seriously cool," I said.

"But still, no reaction." Sabrina took the wand back again. "Try another." Again, we quickly worked our way through the pile. Sabrina told me each wand was for a different type of witch. There was a wand for a Divination Witch, a wide flat stick covered in unusual looking symbols—no reaction. A wand that looked like a splintered piece of flotsam that smelled distinctly of salt, this was for a Sea Witch —once again, no reaction. The last wand was for a Green Witch, a mossy looking stick that Sabrina snatched back as soon as I touched it.

"Well, that's all the wand types," she said.

"Maybe I'm not a witch?" I hazarded. What if this was all a massive mistake and I wasn't meant to be here? I'd probably have to go back to the city, back to my old life. Back to a reality where life didn't seem as fun or warm.

Sabrina laughed. "No, I think there's another answer at play here, one that's much more interesting, though *very* unlikely." Sabrina opened the last box and held up a rather plain looking wand. By comparison of the previous wands this thing looked rather uninspired.

"What's this one?" I asked.

"There are five witch types, but there's also one more, though it's very rare. It's a Prismatic Witch, a witch that can interact with all five magic types freely. This wand contains elements of all the magic types. It might look plain on the outside, but… looks can be deceiving," she said, passing the wand to me.

As I took the wand it lit up immediately, the plain wood surface igniting in shimmering scales of pink, blue, green, yellow, and red. Light itself seem to come out of the wand, and I felt its warmth through my fingertips. "This is the reaction…" I realized, looking up at the colored light illuminating Sabrina's enamored face. From her expression alone I could tell this was something out of the ordinary.

"Dude, I can't actually believe it," she said, her eyes wide in amazement. "You're a Prismatic Witch. I've never met one before!"

"Wait, this is a rare thing?" I asked. "Is there something wrong with me?"

Sabrina shook her head quickly. "What? Zora, no. This is a good thing! There's never been a Prismatic Witch around here. Heck… I don't think there's currently a living one in America! There's one in South Africa apparently. Maybe one in Scotland too? And then there's also Honey Sparks, but, ugh—she is the worst."

"Honey Who?"

"This Australian witch. She's pretty much like the most powerful witch alive today, and she's super beautiful and talented at everything. She has a dreamlike life and like a million jillion followers on all the internet things."

"Ah, so we hate her out of jealousy," I said with a slight smile. I'd known plenty of people like that in my lifetime. The beautiful talented freaks that landed the superstar spouses, mega mansions and riches galore.

"Pretty much, but Zora, the fact that you are a Prismatic Witch is a *big* freaking deal. Wait until Zelda and Celeste find out about this; they're going to freak!"

That all sounded great and all, but right now I was still doubting the accuracy of Sabrina's assessment. I somehow punched myself in the face this morning when turning over to hit snooze; it seemed very unlikely I was meant to be some great and powerful witch.

"Listen this all sounds great and all, but how am I meant to defend myself if I don't know any magic? Am I even allowed to do any spells without formal training?"

"That is where cantrips come in," Sabrina said through a broad grin.

"Cantrip?" I asked. "What the heck is that?"

"Come on," Sabrina said enthusiastically, jumping to her feet.

CHAPTER 17

I followed Sabrina out the back of her apartment. She had a nice little back garden, with a decent sized lawn and tall flowery trees bordering the fences.

"So, there are kind of like levels to spells, but nothing super official," Sabrina said. "But if we broke them down into levels then a level one spell is something quite small, not dramatic or super powerful."

"And a cantrip? What's that?"

"A cantrip is kind of like a training wheels spell. I guess you could call it level zero. They're super weak, and every witch starts learning magic by learning cantrips. The good thing is they're so lightweight they don't take much power, so you can pretty much cast them all day long and not lose your magical reserves."

"Magical reserves?" I asked.

"Whoa, they really told you nothing, huh?" Sabrina said. "Every witch has a limited amount of magic she can do each day, kind of like a car's fuel tank. When that tank is empty, the car stops. When we go to sleep that tank fills up overnight."

"I wish that happened with cars," I joked.

Sabrina smiled. "Okay, lesson number zero of being a witch, where do you put your wand?"

"In my pocket?" I asked uncertainly.

"Nope," Sabrina said with a grin. She lifted both her hands up pinched her finger and thumb together and pressed them against her palm. All of a sudden, she pulled a wand from nowhere; it was like it had appeared from her hand. I blinked several times while trying to figure out how she just did that.

"That was some seriously impressive sleight of hand."

"Sleight," Sabrina said.

"I am... confused," I revealed.

"What you just saw was *sleight*; it's an ability that all witches have. Have you ever heard people talking about auras?" Sabrina asked.

"Yes, up until now I kind of assumed it was all doo hickey. I'm guessing they're real though."

"You're right, they *are* real, but they're not actually what people think they are. An aura is kind of like a pocket of energy that surrounds everyone, even non-magical people! Witches have the ability to use *sleight* to access that pocket of energy. It's standard practice for a good witch to hide her wand in her aura using her power of slight."

Sabrina pressed the wand against her palm again and sure enough it disappeared.

"That is seriously messing with my mind," I laughed.

"You try," she encouraged. "Hold your wand against your palm and just try to feel your aura, it will feel like an area of dense air around your body. You know how to feel for magic, right?"

"The fuzzy fingertip thing?" I asked.

Sabrina nodded. "Exactly, it's the same sort of thing. Take a deep breath and try it out; I bet you get it on your first try."

I followed Sabrina's instructions and watched in amazement as my wand disappeared through my hand. I was about to ask where it went, but then my vision blurred slightly, and I saw a hazy image of the wand suspended in the air alongside my hand. As I moved my hand the wand followed, like suspended in gelatin.

"I can see it!" I said in amazement.

"Of course you can see it. Now auras aren't super strong so they can't hold a lot of physical weight. Anything more than a few pounds and you'll just start dropping stuff. The good thing is that when you have an item stored in your aura no one else can see it, and no one else can access it either."

"This is seriously cool," I said. I recalled when I first walked into the bakery and saw Zelda pull her wand from her outfit. "What about Zelda?" I asked. "When I first met her, her wand was in her pocket."

"Yeah, Zelda is seriously lazy, and look where that gets her. She's broken like three wands in the last year. So, let's move onto cantrips." Once again Sabrina made her wand appear from her hand. I copied her, retrieving mine also, still feeling a little amazed I could do something like this. "Now I can give you a little book on the known cantrips, there's about fifty in all, and they all do different things."

"Fifty?!" I remarked. "How am I supposed to remember all that?"

"Honestly? You don't. Chances are you're probably not even going to use most of them. I don't even think I've done them all; some are very specific and don't have much practical use. The easy ones to remember, and the ones that people most often start, with are the elemental cantrips. There's fire."

Sabrina drew a tight circle in the air with her wand and a small flame appeared on the tip, not much bigger than a lighter. "How do I do that?" I asked.

"Just think of fire. It will come," she said.

I tried it, and sure enough a little spout of flame came out the end of my wand. Whereas Sabrina's flame was strong and bright, mine was a little dull ball of flickering blue, like a candle that was about to go out.

"Not bad!" she encouraged. "Then we have ice." Sabrina placed the wand against the palm of her hand and a small but perfectly square ice cube appeared there. I tried again, making a small, jagged ball of ice not much bigger than a marble. "Wind, though you can't do much more with it than blow out a candle." To illustrate that, Sabrina produced a lit candle from thin air and extinguished it with a small puff of air from her wand. She relit it and then had me try. The flame fluttered before going out again.

"Guess I know how I'm blowing out my birthday cake this year," I joked.

"Oh, in addition to ice there is water." She held her wand over a plant and a few drops of water came out. I copied her. "And there is earth." Sabrina knelt by a flowerbed and pointed her wand at the soil. Some invisible force gently nudged the soil around. I copied her also.

"This is so cool," I remarked.

"I'm glad you think so! Now admittedly the elemental cantrips aren't much good for defense magic, but there are two more I can think of that might come in handy. One is called *voice*, and the other is called *force*."

"I'm all ears," I said, standing back up with Sabrina.

"Voice basically takes your thoughts, sends it down your wand, and into the wand of another witch."

"Telepathic communication?" I asked.

"Yup," Sabrina said with a knowing smile. "Pretty cool, huh? The one downside is that any witch nearby will pick up those thoughts; it's kind of like a radio. The range is limited too. Anyone outside of a room is unlikely to pick it up. Let's try. What message am I sending?" Sabrina held her wand to her fingertip and looked at me. A moment later two words appeared in my mind.

Freaky, huh?

"That is super weird," I said, laughing nervously at the strangeness of hearing someone else's voice in my mind.

"It is a little unusual, yes, but it can also come in super handy. One little note to that spell, if your wand is touching another witch's, you can communicate telepathically with them, and no one else can hear. Want to try and send something?"

I placed my wand against my fingertip and willed a message over to Sabrina. *Am I coming in clear?*

"Crystal clear," she said, smiling. "Again, voice is unlikely to be a defensive asset, but you never know when it might come in handy. Finally, that brings us to force, and I think this is your best self-defense as a witch with no formal training. Force allows you to conjure up a projectile of energy. Observe."

Sabrina turned to face the back of her garden, curled up her body like she was about to make first pitch and then she let it rip. The movement ended with her wand hand stretched in the direction of the fence, where a baseball-sized-hole exploded a second later. It was like she had literally pitched a ball through the fence at speed.

"Holy moly!" I said. "What an arm!"

She smiled, waved her wand at the fence and the hole repaired itself. "That's another cantrip, *prestidigitate*, but we'll get to that another time. Wanna try and take a chunk out of my fence?"

I 'stepped up to the plate' and tried to copy Sabrina's action. As I concentrated, it was almost like I could feel a ball of condensed air building in my hand. I threw out my wand hand and a moment later I heard something hit the fence. There was no hole, but I'd definitely thrown something.

"Ta-da!" she said triumphantly. "Thus completes our crash course on cantrips. Sorry I can't do much more than that."

"No. This has been great," I said honestly. "I mean you straight up blew a hole through your fence with that force cantrip. I could defend myself with something like that!"

"Well, hey, feel free to hang out and practice a bit more if you like. I can repair any damage to the fence, so don't sweat it, and I'll—" Just then a small bell over Sabrina's back door started ringing. "Ah, that's my cue to head back into the shop. Looks like I've got customers. Just come back in once you're done, alright?"

"Alrighty. Thanks, Sabrina."

For the next twenty minutes or so I stayed in the back garden by myself, mostly practicing the force cantrip as it seemed like my best option for defending myself in a pinch. I lost count of how many invisible projectiles I sent hurling at that fence, but with each new try my efforts seemed to hit harder, the wood rattling louder each time.

I didn't get to a point where I could blow a hole through the fence, but the sound of the impact alone told me I had made some progress. The cantrip already felt much stronger, even after just twenty minutes of practice. Sabrina came back at the end of those twenty minutes and watched me.

"Very good," she observed. "You've already come on a long way! Here, let's try some target practice."

Sabrina dragged an old bench to the end of the garden and put some rusted tin cans upon it. We both took turns blasting the cans off, laughing loudly as we sent each one flying. I felt like a teenager throwing rocks into a lake. It was just good fun, and it was nice spending the time with Sabrina too.

"Well, I think you're definitely equipped to look after yourself now," she said after five minutes or so of blasting cans. "I release you from my tutelage, oh great student."

"Thanks," I chuckled.

We both headed back through Sabrina's apartment and into her shop. I used my *sleight* to hide my wand and looked around at Sabrina's shop before I prepared to leave. "Thanks for everything," I said. "This has been the most I've learned about magic so far. I mean Constance taught me some things about being a kitchen witch, but now I've got a wand, and I can do actual magic!"

"Hey, you're getting there," Sabrina said with a chuckle. "I won't be surprised if you're teaching me a trick or two before long. Being a Prismatic Witch is a big deal, Zora. It won't be long before your power really starts to grow. Man, I can't wait to see the look on Celeste and Zelda's face when I tell them!"

"Do you guys want to come over later?" I asked. "We can have dinner and all that jazz."

"I think Celeste mentioned something about having dinner at her place," Sabrina said, wrinkling her nose as she tried to recall. "My sister can be annoying, but she's a darn good cook, so it's a worthwhile trade-off."

I laughed. "Hey, you're all great in my book. I never had friends or family growing up. I'm really starting to love it here."

"Just watch out for that hot psycho biker, eh?" Sabrina said and raised her brows. "Or whoever this mysterious poisoner is."

"Ain't that the truth? Alright, I'm going to hit the road and head over to the hospital, see if I can dig up any clues there. I guess I'll see you later at Celeste's place. Should I bring anything?"

"Just your sweet old self. Prepare yourself, once Celeste and Zelda find out about your powers, they're going to totally start fangirling over you. I mean I'm finding it pretty hard to hold back myself."

"I almost feel like a celebrity," I joked, expecting Sabrina to laugh as well. Instead, she looked back at me and nodded, a serious expression on her face.

"Yeah, we should possibly look into getting you a security detail or something. Once this news properly gets out into the witching community it's going to bring a *lot* of attention to Compass Cove." Sabrina snapped out of whatever she was imagining and forced a smile. "I'm sure it'll be fine!"

"Well, you get zero points for that convincing performance," I laughed. "Right, really got to go, see you later."

I left the shop and climbed back into my car, pulling back onto the road and following my phone's directions for the hospital. It seemed crazy to think a trip to a magic shop would better prepare me for a murder investigation than a trip to the police station, but I guess that was the life I was living now.

I now had a wand at my disposal, and if anyone wanted to give me trouble, I could hurl some invisible baseball-sized projectiles their way. Not enough to do any real damage, but having been hit by a few baseballs at full speed during gym class, I can attest those things do hurt!

While driving, another thought lingered on my mind though, and surprisingly it wasn't worry of Hudson being on the loose. He was connected to all this somehow, that was for sure, but whether or not he was a danger to me remained to be seen. Something told me we were going to meet again. If he was a threat, I'd be ready for him.

The thing clouding my thoughts was the revelation back at Sabrina's shop. I was a Prismatic Witch, a witch that could interact with the five main different types of magic. Sabrina said there were only a handful of other witches in the world at the moment with that power, so it really was a rare thing.

Upon leaving the shop I didn't fail to notice that silent expression in her eye, an unspoken concern that suggested this revelation wasn't all good news. Sabrina seemed pretty sure this was going to bring a big spotlight upon me and Compass Cove.

It looked like things were only going to get stranger around here.

CHAPTER 18

Compass Cove Hospital was a surprisingly modern looking building, a large angular brick that was all glass, steel, and right angles. It looked more like an airport than a hospital, and as I walked inside, I found myself impressed with the size and cleanliness. I approached the main desk and a young man looked up at me.

"Morning, how may I help you?" he said.

"I need to speak with Colin please."

"Colin who?" he asked, prompting me for a surname.

"I uh—I don't actually have a surname," I said, realizing my faux pas.

"Lady, this is a hospital. Do you know how many Colins we might have here at a given time? Are you a relative of the patient?"

"Oh, he's not a patient, he works here, in the hospital pharmacy." I went to hold up my 'Police Station Guest' badge, but the young man at the reception replied before I could.

"Down to the bank of elevators on that wall that way," he said, leaning forward and pointing right, to the far end of the building. "Up to the third floor and follow the signs."

"Oh, thanks!" I said. "I uh, have a badge—" I said, waving the badge so he could see it.

"That's... very nice?" he said unsurely, looking at me like I was a child. I already knew the lanyard was absolutely useless. I don't know what I thought this was going to achieve; I guess I just didn't think it would be this easy getting in to see Colin.

"I'll just hurry along now," I said, my cheeks turning red with embarrassment as I quickly made my way to the elevators. The hospital was quite busy, a constant stream of patients, visitors, doctors, nurses, and other hospital staff all walking in varying directions. I approached the nearest elevator, hit the call button, and the doors opened with a ping.

Inside, there was a hospital porter and a huge man in a wheelchair with no legs. The porter slowly pushed the man out and I stepped to the side.

"Twinkies," the huge man in the wheelchair said as he passed.

"I beg your pardon?" I asked.

"Twinkies!" he repeated. "My one vice. Lost my legs over them! Diabetes! Don't make my mistake! Limit yourself to three a day!"

"I'll uh... keep that in mind," I said in bewilderment, stepping into the elevator and hitting the button. I watched the man wheel away as the doors closed. "That was odd," I muttered to myself. I mean I like a Twinkie as much as the next gal, but I've not had one in several years.

"You're telling me," a voice said from behind me. I was definitely the only person in the elevator when the doors closed, so I screamed, jumped through the air to the corner, and had my fists up, ready to fight.

It was Constance.

"Are you kidding me?!" I raged, looking at the translucent blue figure of my dead aunt. "What did I tell you about sneaking up on me?!"

"I might be mistaken here, but you said something about 'Keep doing it, it's hilarious when you do that, Constance,'" Constance said with a wicked grin.

"Did I miss a memo or something? Do you get closer to life with every year you take off mine?" I lowered my arms and breathed out the adrenaline.

"Oh, don't be a spoilsport, Zora. I was always a practical joker when I was alive. I've got to get my kicks from somewhere now I'm dead. It gets awful boring floating around after a while. Even spying on the men down at the gym gets old."

"I knew it!" I said, jabbing a finger in her direction.

Constance smiled and rolled her eyes. "Yes, well, here I am following you again. How are things going, catch my killer yet?"

"No, I'm just on the way to speak to Colin at the pharmacy now actually. If we're lucky we might be able to identify the pharmacist thief from the surveillance footage. That might tell us who your killer is."

Constance clapped her hands excitedly. "Ooh, could we perhaps be reaching the thrilling grand reveal!"

"That remains to be seen. Now if you're going to shadow me then I kindly ask you to cut the jump scares and keep the chatter to a minimum," I said, laying down the ground rules for having a ghostly companion.

"I can do that," she reasoned. The elevator doors dinged open, and I stepped out, walking over to a large sign on the opposite wall to look for the pharmacy. After only a few paces Constance started up. "You know I've been thinking about Bruce Willis today—"

"Na-ah!" I said, turning on my heels to face her. There was no one else around at the moment, so I had to address Constance while I could. "What did I just say? I've got to pay attention here, Constance. I can't focus on things if you're whittering away in my ear about John McClane's abs."

"What about his arms?" I tilted my head and raised my brows, indicating I wasn't in the mood for her games. Constance pouted and crossed her arms. "Well, you're no fun."

"The first one," I said before resuming my path to the sign.

"What did you say?" she asked while floating after me.

"The first film is clearly the best of the original trio. That's what you were building up to, wasn't it?"

"How did you know?!"

"I saw Celeste and Zelda at the café. They already told me about your visit," I said.

"Those humbugs, stealing all my conversation topics from me!"

"Alright now shush up, people are coming in this way, and I can't be seen talking to myself. We can talk properly later, okay?"

"Fine," Constance sulked. "You are right though, the first one is the best, hands down."

"Oh, totally."

The huge board in front of me had hundreds and hundreds of rows upon it, all with different colored backgrounds. Names of hospital wards with arrows pointing in various directions. It was a confusing mess, but after ten seconds or so of staring I found the arrow for the hospital pharmacy.

A few minutes later I finally reached the pharmacy after weaving through corridors and around turns. A set of propped open wooden double doors led into a large waiting room, where about five or six people were sitting and waiting for their prescriptions. I approached the reception desk, which was currently empty, and I rang a bell. A silver-haired woman appeared.

"Yes?" she asked.

"Hi, I'm Zora Wick. I'm here to see Colin; is he around?"

"Hang on, let me check." The woman disappeared again, and Colin popped out of the door almost straightaway.

"Zora! You came!"

"Did you think I was going to stand you up? I'm trying to find my aunt's murderer."

Colin chuckled. "Listen, it's my break in five minutes. Why don't you take a seat and then we can talk, okay?"

"Alrighty," I said. I chose a seat in the corner and grabbed an old magazine from the coffee table in front of me. I'd picked up a six-year-old copy of *Quilters Quarterly,* which was dog-eared and close to falling to pieces. Constance, who was staying surprisingly silent, sat down beside me and crossed her legs while leaning in to read my magazine.

"It's true you know," she said casually while reading over my shoulder. "Mitered Binding really isn't as difficult as everyone makes it out to be. It's also the far superior method."

"Just for the record, I don't know anything about quilts," I mumbled under my breath. "I'm not exactly spoilt for choice for reading material."

"Oh, quilting can be quite the rush," Constance said. "You should consider it. I learned it from Millicent."

I turned my head and looked up at Constance, the name ringing a faint bell. "Sabrina mentioned something about a Millicent before. She said you used to be her apprentice and inherited the bakery from her?"

"Oh yes, Millicent was a fantastic baker, better than me, that's for sure! Great quilter too. I can't understate the adrenaline one gets from finishing a good quilt. Better than sex I tell you."

I put the magazine down and pressed my lips together. "Do you know where the ear doctors are located in this hospital?"

"No," Constance said with a bemused smile. "Why?"

"I'd like to pierce both my eardrums, so I never hear you talk about sex again."

Constance rolled her eyes. "You young people, all prudes! It's just nature, Zora. I lived through the seventies; I went to Woodstock! Let me tell you, down in the mud with twenty other people, it was hard to tell where one body ended and the other began!"

I stared ahead, trying to erase that image from my head. "You know, it's funny. I kind of asked you to stop talking about that, and you just doubled down."

My ghostly aunt cackled and winked at me. "If I can't embarrass a niece every now and then what am I good for?!"

"Alright, Zora. I'm all yours!" Colin said as he ducked under the counter and came over to see me. "Are you okay? You look a little bit pale."

"I'm fine," I said, taking a deep breath and putting the quilting magazine down. "Just reading about the daredevil world of quilting. It's really white-knuckle stuff."

Colin chuckled. "I'll bet. Follow me this way; my office is just down here."

I followed Colin down a short corridor, halfway along which he stopped and tapped a keycard against a scanner. The door unlocked and Colin went inside, leading me into the back of the pharmacy. "I just want to show you something for illustration purposes first," he said, walking me over to a solid-looking door that was locked with a padlock *and* a key scanner. "That's the drugstore in there. It's a small room, but the drugs in there are worth millions."

"That explains the security then," I said, regarding the padlock and the keycard scanner.

"The padlock has always been there; the scanner is a recent addition. Come, my office is this way." Colin walked back out of the pharmacy and down the hall to a small room with a desk and a computer. There wasn't much space in here, and the few pieces of furniture really dominated the small space. Colin sat and invited me to do so too as he unlocked his computer.

"This isn't going to be one of those situations where I ask for surveillance footage and it's been deleted, is it?" I asked warily.

"Quite the contrary," Colin said. "Being a hospital, we have strict federal codes we have to follow when it comes to the storage of security footage. All surveillance has to be stored at a minimum for ninety days."

"But the break-in was over a year ago," I said.

"Of course, but we kept the footage from the break-in for insurance purposes. I have a copy on my computer; security gave it to me."

"Well, that's a relief," I commented. So often you heard stories about businesses wiping their surveillance footage at the end of a day. I understand that storage isn't cheap, and you're not likely to keep footage if there wasn't an incident, but so many things go on in the background, I always wonder how many more crimes might be solved if people held onto footage for a little longer.

"Won't be a moment," Colin chuckled awkwardly after a minute or two of silent searching. "I could have sworn I had the file here somewhere."

MARA WEBB

I felt myself grow slightly apprehensive as Colin struggled to locate the file. My mind immediately started jumping to conclusions. What if the thief had returned here and wiped the footage, knowing someone was looking into the case?

What if Colin was the culprit, and he had wiped the footage to cover himself?

Was I in danger in here, alone in this room with a man I barely knew?

Looking down at the hand he had on the computer mouse I noticed a gold signet ring with a heart imprinted upon it. In an effort to distract myself I commented on it. "Nice ring," I said.

"Oh? Thanks," Colin said, glancing at the ring momentarily.

"Girlfriend? Wife? Overly affectionate mother?"

He laughed. "I guess girlfriend would be the word. Ah! Here we are, found it. I cleaned up my computer a couple of weeks ago and moved some things around." Colin pivoted the monitor around and I leaned forward too. He hit the play button and the surveillance clip started.

The camera was situated in the pharmacy, pointed right at the padlocked door Colin had shown me only moment ago. Though there was a padlock, there was no keycard scanner. "This footage is amazingly crisp," I said. "Whenever you see clips like this on TV, they look like postage stamps."

"Federal mandates," he said with another knowing smile. "All surveillance footage has to be captured in high definition, and there's even night vision on these cameras too, though the pharmacy has motion-activated lights. The break-in happened just after two in the morning. Here we are."

The footage had been in black and white up until now, but the screen suddenly went bright white as the motion-activated lights came on. The image adjusted quickly, and a hooded figure emerged from the left. They went straight over to the padlocked door and hunched over it, their back to the camera.

"They picked the lock?" I asked Colin.

"No, keep watching," he said.

After about thirty seconds the hooded figure stepped back from the padlock, crouched down, and pulled off their backpack. I realized they had a spray canister of some sort in their hand. They stashed the canister in the backpack and pulled out a—

"Is that a hammer?" I asked in confusion. A moment later the hooded figure smashed the hammer against the padlock. The lock broke and dropped to the ground. "Hang on, what just happened there?" I asked. Colin paused the video.

"It's not so clear on video, but the thief froze the lock with that spray canister. Then they hit the lock with a hammer and the lock shattered."

"Talk about a sophisticated operation," I said. This wasn't just a junkie breaking in for a quick fix, that was for sure.

"Right?" Colin agreed. He hit play again and the figure dashed through the door and another camera angle appeared, showing the thief inside the drug storage room. "Looks like they knew exactly where they were going." The thief moved quickly and precisely, grabbing one small glass vial of the fentanyl before darting back out again. It was on their way out from the locked door that I finally saw their face for the first time. Colin paused the video.

"The most annoying thing is that we got a clear shot of the guy's face," Colin sighed. "But nothing ever came of it. Here you are though. This is the thief. You reckon you can identify the guy?" he asked.

I sat there, my mouth hanging open as I stared at the face already known to me. "Uh yeah... in fact I know who this is."

"You do?!" Colin said in alarm.

"Yeah. His name is Nick. Or it *was* at least."

"Wait, was?"

"He died yesterday in the park," I told Colin. I stood up quickly as I prepared to go. Jerk wad biker was the fentanyl thief. In my mind this all but confirmed the bikers had something to do with Constance's death. "I have to go," I said. "I need to look into this."

CHAPTER 19

As soon as I got back to the car, I pulled out my phone and called Linda using the direct line on her business card. She answered after three rings.

"One working in a studio," she said.

"What?!"

"Seven letters down. One working in a studio. What's the answer?"

"I haven't got time for games right now, Linda, I need your help!"

"I know you do, Zora Wick. Just like I knew that you'd be the one calling me. I don't give out my direct line to just anyone, and lo and behold, I give it to you and you're already calling me inside of an hour."

"You told me to call you if I need help, and I do. I've made a break on the case. The person that stole fentanyl from the hospital pharmacy last year was Nick, the biker that died yesterday."

"Now I'll admit that is *very* interesting," Linda said, and she did actually sound quite intrigued. "But we have a strict code of conduct here at the police station. If you scratch my back, I'll scratch yours."

I closed my eyes and imagined hurling my phone through my windshield. Opening them again I saw Constance floating around outside the front of the hospital, dive-bombing at unsuspecting

CAKES TO DIE FOR

people and laughing to herself. They couldn't see her, and she had no effect on them, so she must have been really bored.

"Fine, I'll play your stupid game. Seven letters, right?"

"That's right, cupcake. One working in a studio."

I chewed the fingernails on my left hand while I tried to puzzle the clue out. Nothing was coming to me. "What does that even mean?! It makes no sense!"

"You're telling me, sugar; I've been stuck on this bad boy since you left the station."

My eyes moved back to Constance, who had now grown bored of dive-bombing unaware pedestrians. Two men were painting a section of hospital wall just in front of where I was parked. They were on a platform winched up about twenty feet. Constance was now pretending to teeter off the edge of the platform, looking over to see if I found her constant slapstick attempts in the least bit amusing.

That's when the answer came to me. "It's painter," I said.

"That's it!" Linda shouted excitedly down the phone. "Zora, I just know this is the start of a beautiful working relationship."

"Uh-huh, can you help me now?"

"Of course I can, sugar drop. What do y'all need?"

"Do you have an address on file for this Nick character? I just watched the surveillance footage and it's him. He's the one that stole the fentanyl—things are looking very likely that he killed Constance too. I want to check out his place and see if I can dig up any more concrete clues."

"Makes sense to me..." Linda mused; in the background I heard her fingers clacking over a keyboard. "Let me just see what I can find here." A few moments of silence followed. "Here we go! One address for Nick Largo. 311 Juniper Heights, Aurora Street."

"Excellent. Thanks, Linda. I appreciate it."

"No problem. Are you sure you're going to be okay checking this place out by yourself? I know you think this Nick might have killed your aunt, but I needn't remind you he died in a similar way yesterday. That suggests to me the killer is still out there."

"Yeah, I know," I said, feeling a chill down my spine. "No need to remind me. Don't worry, I can look after myself." Little did Linda know I could use magic to throw invisible baseball-sized objects. As long as this rogue killer was an old rusty can on a wall, I had no problems.

"Don't hesitate to call again if you need my help," Linda advised. "I'm always here for you, Zora."

"Providing I answer your crossword puzzle clues first, right?"

"Hey, nothing in this life is free, kiddo!" she chuckled and ended the call.

I put my phone back in my bag and waved to Constance to signal that I was about to leave. She quickly floated over to the car and through the roof. "Did you see that?" she asked. "I was pretending to fall off that platform up there. It was pretty funny!"

"Yeah, it was a real laugh riot. Listen, I've got the address for this biker guy that robbed the pharmacy. I'm going to go and check out his apartment and see if I can dig up any more evidence. Do you think you'd be able to come along and cover me?"

"Well, if you must know I've got a lot to do today, but I guess I can spare thirty minutes to make sure my niece doesn't get killed."

"What could you possibly have to do today?" I asked her.

"I'll have you know my schedule is very busy!" she said with an offended expression. "I've not yet done my daily lap of the cove, and I was planning on bothering Celeste, Sabrina, and Hermes at least once more before dinnertime."

"We better get a move on then. Do you want to ride in the car?" I paused and considered the question, staring at the woman that was floating halfway through a seat. "*Can* you ride in the car?"

"With effort on my behalf, yes. It's probably easier if I just float up into the air and follow you from above. I can pretend I'm playing a video game and driving the car!"

I stared at my unusual aunt. "Whatever it takes to get through the day. Right, stay close and I'll talk to you when I get there. I'll try and drive slowly so I don't lose you. We're heading for Juniper Heights on Aurora Street."

"I know it. Let's hit the road, baby!"

I left the hospital parking garage and headed west back along Main Street, back in the direction of the bakery and the park in the center of Compass Cove. The directions on my phone had me pass the street for the bakery, and two blocks later I took a right and drove north for a few more streets until taking a left and pulling over just down the road from a large brown brick building that looked like it was straight out of an old movie set in Manhattan.

As I got out of the car, I saw Constance float around the corner and come over to me. It was pretty quiet around here at the moment; most of the building seemed to be residential, and at present we were the only ones on the sidewalk.

"Your rear taillight is out," she commented. "The left one."

"It's not my car; it's a rental." One that was due back at the rental place tomorrow. After that I'd either have to buy a car or figure out the public transport network. "What are the buses like in this town?" I asked Constance as we crossed the street.

"Fairly reliable. There's a subway too, believe it or not. Only six stops on the entire route, but it's a quick way of getting around town."

"You're kidding me!" I said. "How on earth does a town this small have a subway?"

"Back in the eighties the mayor at the time was married to a woman, she was the daughter of travel magnate, Viola Vanhoven. That family owns half the country. To cut a long story short the town ended up getting a pretty good deal for the subway, and the rest is history. The Vanhovens built the station at cost, and to this day the network holds the record for being the smallest metropolitan subway system. We get a lot of tourism off the back of that!" Constance said.

"It seems like Compass Cove is just this boiling pot of bizarre culture."

"That it is, and this place never fails to draw in the crazies. Just look at you; you found your way here!"

"Very funny," I said as we approached the building. "Need I remind you I'm the sucker lured here by you ultimately." Constance winked in amusement but said nothing more.

The front door of Juniper Heights was locked, and there was no sign of anyone in the foyer beyond. On the wall to my right there was a tall intercom panel with buttons for the apartments. I didn't just want to randomly dial an apartment and hope someone would let me in. At the bottom of the panel there was a button that said 'Help', so I pressed it.

"Yes?" a gravelly voice said through a speaker on the panel a moment later.

"Hello," I said. "Who is this?"

"This is Frank, I'm the building superintendent. What do you want?"

"Hi, Frank, my name is Zora Wick. I'm working with Compass Cove PD, pursuing an ongoing murder investigation. I'm here to search the property of one Nick Largo, I believe he lives in apartment..." I paused and checked the address I had written down. "311."

"I see. Do you have a search warrant, Zora Wick?"

"A search warrant?" I repeated, surprised by the question.

"Yes, a search warrant. A legal document granting you access to a private domicile."

"I... do," I lied.

"Alright, hold it up to the camera so I can see it. It's the glass dome at the top of the intercom."

Argh, I should have known that lie wasn't going to work so easily.

"Okay, I actually haven't got a warrant, but Nick Largo is deceased. I don't know if that changes things?" I asked hopefully.

"It does actually. Now I know I have to find a replacement tenant for that apartment, so thanks for letting me know."

I rolled my eyes and sighed. "Listen, mister, this is important business. If you could just let me in and cooperate it would be much appreciated. I have a pass!" I said, holding up the 'Police Station Guest' lanyard.

"That says *Police Station Guest*," Frank said guardedly over the intercom.

"Yes, I know that," I said through my teeth, hating how little I had to work with here. "If you call the station, they will—"

"Listen, Zora Wick," Frank interrupted. "For all I know you're some crazy drug addict looking to break in here to rob the place blind. I'm sorry, but if you're not a resident and you don't have a legal reason to be in this building, you're not coming in. Thanks. Bye."

With Frank's abrupt dismissal the intercom clicked, and I knew the call was over. I tapped my foot in the entrance before turning away and pacing down the sidewalk. "I don't know why I assumed I'd be able to get in here without any trouble," I huffed to Constance.

"Where are you going?! Don't give up that easily! Walk back over there and speak to that super again!" she said.

"And say what? You already heard the man; he's not going to let me in without a warrant."

"He just needs a little persuasion," Constance suggested. "Hit that button again and tell him to let you in, or you'll knock his teeth out!"

I raised my brows at her and rolled my eyes. "Yeah, really helpful, Constance, thanks."

"Oh, I'm kidding! Listen," she said, floating after me as I carried on down the sidewalk. We reached the alleyway at the edge of the building. Constance floated around the front of me, making me stop. "You just have to get a little creative," she said, pointing in the way of the alley. "Let's find a backdoor and use magic to get inside."

"Isn't that breaking and entering?" I asked, knowing full well that it was.

"All great detectives break the law at some point or another; it's all part of the fun! Breaking into places you're not supposed to, snooping around, eavesdropping, walking that thin blue line!"

"I think you're bored and just looking for fun, and your morals are quickly dissolving with each passing day," I said.

"That is... probably true, but let's remember why we're here, Zora. You're trying to solve my murder. Where's your investigative spirit? I thought journalists were supposed to get creative in situations like these! You meet a wall; you jump over it! Surely you must have done stuff like that before when you were studying in college?"

"Well... as a matter of fact you're right. When I broke that case about scholarship fraud, I was poking around quite a few places when

I shouldn't have been. It paid off though; that crooked faculty was cleaned out."

"There it is!" Constance said excitedly. "That renegade street spirit that guides real investigation. Come on, follow me! I'll show you a trick or two. We're not letting this mission end here in a disappointing alleyway!"

"Alright," I sighed. If I was being honest, I didn't want to walk away from this building either before I got some answers. Part of me felt like I should try and play things straight now I had a new life in a new town, but I also had to consider my new family. There was a killer on the loose still, and if I didn't catch them, no one would. I had to do this.

I followed Constance down the alleyway and sure enough we found a service door at the back of the building, though the door was locked. "Take out your wand," Constance said. "You're about to learn something."

"How did you know I have a wand?" I asked.

"I can see it on your aura. All ghosts can see auras."

"Oh, Sabrina didn't tell me that," I said, pinching my fingers against my palm and pulling my wand out with my power of slight.

"Sabrina has been teaching you?" Constance asked.

"Just a little. I stopped over at her place this morning before I went to the hospital. I wanted a way to defend myself; she taught me some cantrips. Elemental stuff and force."

Constance stuck her lip out and nodded her approval. "Good girl. That's about all we can teach you so far, I'm afraid, but it's better than nothing. There is another cantrip that can help you though. It's called *helping hand.*"

"Helping hand? What's that?" I asked.

"Hold up your wand and imagine a hand at the tip. You can lift small objects and move them without touching them." Constance stuck her head through the locked metal door and pulled it back out again. "This is locked with a simple barrel lock. All you have do is turn that lock and you're in. The helping hand can take care of that for you."

"Okay..." I said unsurely, holding up the wand to try the spell out. Before I could, Constance leaned in close to inspect the wand.

"Hold the phone," she said. "What is *this* thing?"

"It's a... wand," I said, wondering if this was some sort of test.

"Zora, I've been a kitchen witch for fifty years, and this ain't no wand for a kitchen witch. What did Sabrina give you? I think you might have picked up the wrong wand."

"Oh, right!" I said, realizing Constance didn't know about our discovery back at Sabrina's shop. "So, it turns out I'm like one of these 'Prismatic Witches', or something like that. Sabrina was making out like it was a really big deal, but—"

Even though Constance was a ghost, it looked like her ghostly hue had just faded rather drastically. She gawped at me in surprise. "I think I have to sit down; I feel a bit dizzy."

"Ghosts can get dizzy?" I asked, watching as Constance floated down to the floor until her legs had disappeared through the ground. She put one hand against her head and stared at me in disbelief.

"Apparently so!" she remarked. "I don't believe it. You're a Prismatic Witch? Really? Zora, do you know how rare that is?"

"Sabrina told me there's like three others in the world right now," I said.

"Uh yeah, this is a massive deal! How are you so calm about this?" Constance had moved on from shock now and was visibly excited, her ghostly hands trembling.

"I know absolutely nothing about this world, so that helps. If Tom Brady walked down this alleyway and you knew nothing about football, you'd think he was just another guy."

"Who?" Constance asked.

"My point exactly," I said. "He's a superstar quarterback. Only a handful of people in the world can throw a ball like him."

"Right, right, a sports analogy. That was always going to go over my head." Constance shook her head slightly, trying to refocus herself. "Okay I'm definitely not over this Prismatic Witch business yet, but we are *definitely* coming back to this later."

"Oh, I imagine we will," I said, sensing this was just the beginning of weird reactions.

"Eyes front, let's focus. If you pay attention to the hand at the end of the wand, you'll notice you can control it with a little effort, like it was a hand of your own. Try it out." I stared at the translucent white hand floating at the end of the wand, and sure enough I could move it with a little practice. The movement was jerky and crude, but I was sure it would get better with time. "Not bad. Now put the hand in the lock, use the fingers to feel for the chamber and turn it until it's open. It's that simple!"

As it turned out, simple wasn't simple at all, and only after ten minutes of trying, three dramatic declarations that it was too hard, and encouragement from Constance, the lock clicked and the door swung open, revealing a dingy stairwell. "I did it!" I said.

Constance winked at me and smiled. "That you did. Now we've got the 'breaking' part out the way let's move on to 'entering.'" Constance floated through the open doorway, and I followed her. I was now officially breaking the law.

Hopefully this paid off.

CHAPTER 20

The dark and dingy stairwell looked like it was some sort of fire evacuation route. It didn't seem like anyone had been in here for some time. As we followed the stairs up, we passed a door on each floor. Nick Largo's apartment was 311, so naturally we continued up until we reached the third floor.

Obstacles were an inherit part of investigation apparently, because as I tried the door, I realized it was locked too. Constance floated through to inspect the other side and came back to my side again to report what she found. "Fire doors, they're locked from this side, but there's a lever on the other side. If you press it in the door will open. Another chance to practice *helping hand!*"

"Great," I muttered under my breath, not really wanting to spend another ten minutes trying to open a door. With little other choice however, I pulled my wand out again, conjured up the little ghostly hand, and focused. Maybe it was lucky because this door didn't actually involve a lock, but it only took me about a minute of trying this time, and I could swear it was getting a little easier to control the individual digits of the hand.

The door swung open, and I crept into the hallway, looking left and right like some thief breaking into a world-class museum. I realized from this point on that if anyone in the hallway saw me, I could pretend I was just another tenant here. Creeping around would only make me look suspicious, so I had to walk like I belonged.

"What are you doing?!" Constance hissed as I started walking normally.

"Blending in," I said. "What looks more suspicious? Some weird girl creeping around corners or acting like I live here?"

Constance considered the question for a second but then nodded. "Fair point, carry on!"

It didn't take long to find Nick's apartment. There was only a dozen or so doors on this story, and 311 was right at the end of the hallway, the last door on the right. "Float through, tell me what the door is like," I said to Constance. She gave me a mock salute and disappeared through the door.

"Aye, aye, captain!" A moment later Constance was back again. "We've got another barrel lock. Shouldn't be difficult for you now that you've mastered *helping hand*."

"Don't make fun," I said disapprovingly. I held up my wand and started working on the lock. Things already felt a little more familiar now on my third try, but these barrel locks were still a lot harder than pushing down a bar on a fire escape door. Still, I did get the door open eventually, and I did do it a little faster. It only took me three or so minutes, which still felt like a lifetime standing out in an open hallway, wondering if someone was going to come out and catch me.

The lock clicked. I pushed the door open and walked slowly inside, my breath held as I quietly closed it behind me. Walking through the hallway was one thing, but now, as I was creeping through another person's apartment, my heart was thumping in my chest. I shouldn't be here, I knew that much, and I couldn't help but feel like I was going to get caught at any moment.

"You know, it just occurred to me; you totally could have just opened the latch on this side with *helping hand*. Would have been much easier than picking a lock," Constance said.

"Well, aren't you bang on time with your useful suggestions."

Constance grinned sheepishly. "I checked the apartment already,"

CAKES TO DIE FOR

she said, and floated around the corner. "No one is in here, you can relax."

I did relax a little, but I still had this tingling feeling on the back of my neck that I was in danger. "I know, I just can't shake this nervous feeling. Let's hurry up and have a look around, see if we can find anything."

I tried to make myself go a little quicker through the apartment. It wasn't very big at all, and it reminded me a lot of my dingy little studio apartment that I had left back in the city. The place was a bit of a mess. Nick Largo was living up the bachelor life apparently.

"I bet it stinks of man in here," Constance said. "I'm glad I can't smell anymore. It stinks right, tell me it stinks."

"There is a certain musk in the air, I'll give you that," I said, grimacing at heaps of clothes on the arms of the sofa. The counters in the small kitchen were awash with dirty plates and takeout containers. I cautiously went into the bedroom, finding an unmade bed, a floor covered with clothes, and piles of boxes stacked in the corner, all full of clutter.

"What are we looking for exactly?" Constance asked.

"To be honest, I don't know. We've pretty much proved Nick was the fentanyl thief now thanks to the surveillance footage, but we still have nothing concrete to connect him to your death." I imagined if Nick was the one that killed Constance, then the prints on the glass jar of fentanyl might be enough to accuse him, but since his death I got the horrible feeling that we still didn't have all the answers.

"Can you make yourself useful and look around too?" I said to Constance, who had mostly been hovering over my shoulder so far. "You can reach hard to access areas more easily than I can."

Constance responded with a surprisingly enthusiastic "Sure!" and floated off to start investigating. I rooted through a couple of boxes that were stacked high in the corner of Nick's bedroom. There were hi-fi systems, wireless headphones, and coffee machines, all sealed in their original packaging. It looked like Nick had more than one illegal hustle going on.

"Found anything?" I called out to Constance. She popped down from the ceiling and shook her head.

"No, there's a small crawl space above the apartment; the entrance is in the living room. I had a quick look around but there's nothing up there apart from some old band posters."

"Anything good?" I asked.

"Nothing. No Donny Osmond at all."

"Yeah, there's a specific type of single man that would horde Donny Osmond posters, and Nick wasn't it." I crouched down to the floor to look under the bed and something caught my attention. There was a black duffel bag, and a part of me knew this bag had what we were looking for. "Hold the phone, Constance. I think I've got something here," I said, pulling out the old duffel bag. It was covered in dust and looked like it had been under the bed for some time.

"What makes you think that's important?" Constance asked. "Looks like an old sack to me."

"I dunno. I have this feeling, like a tingling down the back of my neck."

"Ah, that's your intuition," Constance remarked. "Witches have great intuition, a silent and innate sense that guides them. Yours must be pretty developed; it usually is in witches that learn magic later on."

I unzipped the dusty duffle bag, coughing a little bit as dust wafted through the air. Inside I saw three things: a spray canister labeled 'Spray Ice', a stack full of cash that had to amount to $50,000 at least, and a weird shiny black orb that was pulsating with a deep blue light.

"Holy mackerel!" Constance said, looking at the mysterious orb. "What the heck is that thing?!" I leaned in closer and felt a deep bass note vibrating from the orb. It was unlike anything I'd ever seen before. Something told me not to touch it, but I hovered my hands over the orb and felt no magical presence.

"It's not magic, right?" I asked Constance. I already knew I could feel no magic, but for some reason I felt like I had to double-check with her.

"No way, that's something else altogether. My gut is telling me to stay the heck away from it!"

"Same here. Well, we've found the canister of Spray Ice at least;

that all but confirms Nick was the fentanyl thief, as for the money he's a crook, so that seems reasonable enough. This orb thing though, I have—"

"Quiet!" Constance hissed, her face suddenly filling with dread. Her eyes shot to the wall, looking in the direction of the living room. "There's someone here! I just heard something!"

All of a sudden, my heart was in the back in my throat, a drum beating so loudly through my temples that I felt like I was going to throw up. I readied my wand and prepared to start hurling invisible baseball-sized projectiles.

Constance stuck her head through the wall, then yanked it back just as quick. Even though she was invisible to others and couldn't be heard she was caught up in the moment. "Living room!" she mouthed, pointing through the wall.

"How many?" I whispered. She held up a finger to indicate 'one'.

"Man!" she mouthed back. "Big man!"

Just great.

Part of me wanted to roll under the bed and hide, but there was so much clutter under there I couldn't fit anyway. Besides, I was a witch now. I didn't have to hide in the shadows anymore; I could defend myself. I could fight back.

I crept over to the door while Constance remained frozen in the corner. It would be really handy if she could be my eyes and let me know what this other intruder was up to, but I guess I had to make do by myself. As I reached the door I paused and held my wand in the air, holding my breath as I listened for sound of the other intruder.

Very quietly I heard footsteps moving over the floorboards. Whoever was in here knew they weren't alone. There was nothing else for it. I could creep around or jump out and take them by surprise.

Here went nothing. One, two, three!

I jumped out from the doorway, ready to make my attack. My plan was to blast the other intruder with one of my projectiles, and after that I didn't have much more of a plan. Run away? Keep blasting them? I don't know—I probably should have thought it through more.

What actually happened was a little bit different. I jumped through the door, ready to attack, and as soon as I did the other intruder came round the corner and we crashed together. I screamed, bounced off their huge frame, and hit the floor.

As I fell back through the air screaming, I fired off a force projectile from my wand, but as the cantrip activated I immediately knew I'd cast something significantly larger than a baseball. I felt a block of force burst out the end of the wand, and it was at least the size of a small end table. It hit the other intruder square in the chest and sent them flying across the apartment and crashing into the wall in the living room.

They dropped to the ground and then there was silence for a few seconds. We were both groaning, and as I scrambled to my feet I realized the back of my head felt hot. Placing a hand to it I found a little bit of blood. I turned around and saw that I'd hit the corner of a small cabinet on the wall outside Nick's door.

"Sweet baby Moses..." the other intruder groaned. Looking over, I saw them on all fours, struggling to get up to their feet. I'd knocked the wind out of them.

"Stop right there!" I demanded. "What do you think you're doing in—wait, you?!" I got closer, my wand held out in front of me like a gun. The other intruder lifted their head and as they looked up, I saw who it was. It was Hudson. "What are you doing here?!"

"Getting the crap kicked out of me apparently," he said, pushing himself onto his knees. He looked back at the wall he'd hit. There was a hole in the drywall from his body. "And I might ask you the same question. What are *you* doing here?"

"I'm here on official police business!" I said, my other hand scrambling for my useless 'Police Station Guest' lanyard and holding it up. "I should have known I'd find you here. What are you doing? Destroying evidence? Come to finish me off?!" I had to admit I was a little jumpy, and I was waving my wand wildly around as I tried to contain my nerves. I kept it pointed at Hudson despite my panic.

He eyed the wand and just laughed. "So, you're a witch. I should have figured. That would explain the crazy vibes I got from you."

"Crazy?!" I said. "What on earth do you mean, I'm not—wait a second, you know about witches?" Even in my moment of fraught panic I knew from my witch sense that Hudson wasn't a magical person.

Hudson pushed himself onto his feet and dusted himself off. "Look, you need to get out of here. It's not safe. Someone killed Nick and I'm trying to figure out what happened. The killer is still on the loose, whoever they are."

"Ha!" I laughed. "Nice try. But you are obviously the killer. Why else would you be creeping around here! The police arrested you!"

"No, they didn't."

Damn, Linda *had* confirmed that much with me. "Well, they put you in the police car. I saw it!"

"My friend just died; they were making sure I was okay."

"I—" I opened my mouth and closed it again. "That does sound sort of reasonable, I guess. But you're still hiding something from me!"

Hudson laughed. "Coming from the girl that is also sneaking around an apartment. From where I'm standing, you're just as suspicious. Your aunt dies, you inherit her bakery, you turn up, just 'happen' to find the poison that killed her, and then my friend dies a day later."

Once again, my mouth was hanging open; somehow, I found myself momentarily speechless. I had to concede that things did *not* look good for me. "I can't believe I'm saying this, but you're actually right."

He just laughed again. For a man that had just been blown across the room he was irritatingly smug, and even though he was covered in drywall dust he still looked amazing. "For what it's worth, I don't think you're the person I'm tracking down, but you *should* get out of here now, it's not safe and—" All of a sudden Hudson jerked his head in the direction of the front door and his eyes went wide. "Get down!"

In that split second, I looked over at the doorway and saw a figure holding a gun. Before I could do anything else there was a flash of light, and two loud bangs. Hudson dived through the air, and we crashed to the ground.

"You saved me!" I gasped, swallowing down the nerves in my throat as I stared up at the huge man lying on top of me, his body surrounding me like a cage. Perhaps I should have been more concerned that someone had just tried to shoot us, but I was a little caught up in my physical proximity to the hot life-saving biker.

"Pay me back later!" he said. As much as I wanted that moment to linger, Hudson jumped to his feet and vaulted over the sofa. "Stay there; they're getting away!" he ordered. As he hit the ground he ran for the door and disappeared around the corner.

I quickly jumped to my feet too and saw Constance staring in amazement. "Wow, he is like, super-hot. Hey, where are you going? He said to stay put!"

"Uh yeah, I'm not doing that!" I said, running out into the hallway to help Hudson. As I went around the corner, I heard two more gunshots ring out. Hudson was about halfway down the long corridor, and he dropped to the ground. The mysterious shooter disappeared around the corner, then they were gone. "Hudson!" I shouted. I ran over to him and dropped to my knees, he had one hand on his shoulder and was bleeding. "You've been hit!"

"I'm fine," he grimaced. "It's just my shoulder." I took his other hand and squeezed it. "You're going to be okay; I won't leave you." I pulled out my phone and called 911.

"What's your emergency?" the person on the other end of the line asked.

"I need an ambulance now; there's been a shooting at Juniper Heights on Aurora Street!"

"Relax, I already said I'm fine," Hudson repeated. "Is it me, or is the hallway spinning?" Hudson was blinking heavily, his pupils dilated.

"Stay with me, Hudson. I'm not letting you go this easily!"

"I'll go and find Sabrina!" Constance shouted. "She'll be able to help!" With that she darted off through the ceiling, leaving me holding Hudson's hand. I noticed my knees felt wet and saw blood pooling on the floor under Hudson.

This wasn't good. We needed a miracle.

CHAPTER 21

The hospital waiting room was stark and clinical. Sabrina and Constance were with me; it had been an hour since Hudson had been taken into surgery.

"Hey, sit back and relax," Sabrina said, for what had to be the hundredth time. "I already told you everything is going to be okay. I got there before the paramedics and managed to stop the bleeding with my magic. He'll be fine, really."

I nodded at Sabrina, but I didn't sit back or relax. I was on the edge of my seat, rocking back and forth, my hands fidgeting restlessly in my lap. "Yeah, he's probably fine. He's not dead, right? Because if he *was* dead then it would totally be my fault."

"From the sounds of things neither of you were supposed to be there. You knew the risks, and I'm sure Hudson did too," Sabrina said. Despite her logic I still felt like this was my fault.

"He saved my life," I said. "I'd probably be dead if it wasn't for him."

An old man in overalls came around the corner, followed by a younger man who was all brawn. The old man had a thick silver moustache and a cowboy hat, his thumbs were tucked into his belt. He reminded me of some old-time cowboy or a prospector. "Alright," he said, "Where's Nancy Drew?" He took one look at me and nodded. "I don't know your face, so it must be you. I'm Sheriff Burt. My wife, Linda, tells me you're our latest member down at the police station?" he said with a light chuckle. He held out his hand and I shook it.

"I got the guest lanyard and everything," I joked back absently.

"Well, that about makes it official," the younger man in overalls said. Both him and Burt were covered head to toe in dirt. "I'm Wayne, one of the other officers down at the station." Wayne paused and gave Sabrina an awkward nod. "Sabrina."

"Wayne," Sabrina said back, her eyes looking down at the floor.

Weird.

"Why are you both covered in dirt?" I asked.

"Clearing that road," Burt said. "It's an all-hands-on deck kind of operation at the moment. We've been at it for weeks and there's no end in sight. Listen, Zora, is it? I need to ask you a few quick questions about what happened here. Linda already told me she gave you the go-ahead to check the apartment. What's the story from there?"

I recounted the story to Burt, leaving out any parts that mentioned magic. I didn't tell him how I'd somehow blasted Hudson across the apartment, or how Sabrina arrived before the medics to help save Hudson's life. Both the men listened as I told the story.

"Did you get a look at the shooter?" Wayne asked as I reached the end. "Any visual information you could give us to narrow down a suspect?"

I shook my head. "Not really, no, sorry. Everything happened so fast. All I know is they looked big, and they could move fast."

"Shame they've got an itchy trigger finger," Burt said as he wrote something down in his notepad. "The Compass Cove Reapers could use a new linebacker." Wayne nodded his head in agreement.

"Alright, Zora, if you remember anything else then you come and find us. It looks like we might have a dangerous person on the loose, so you should probably hang back now and leave the investigating to us. We're taking a break from clearing the road to catch this individual."

"Got it," I said, glad I wasn't alone in this anymore. Burt and

Wayne excused themselves and left the waiting room. As soon as they left, a doctor came in holding a clipboard.

"You're the girlfriend, right?" he said, looking at me.

"Uh—" I began.

"Yes, yes she is," Sabrina said quickly.

"Alright. Good news, he's doing fine. He was lucky and unlucky. I'll preface this by saying there's no good place to get hit by a bullet. Now if you had to pick one place the shoulder is usually the best place to get hit, but the bullet just about tagged his subclavian artery. That's why he was bleeding out so fast. I don't know what slowed down the bleeding, but he's lucky to be alive."

I let out a deep breath and dropped my head into my hands. "Oh, thank goodness." Sabrina placed her hand on my back reassuringly.

"Would you like to come and see him?" the doctor asked. I looked up at him in surprise.

"I can do that?"

He laughed awkwardly. "It's common practice for family or partners. You *are* his girlfriend, right?" he asked with an air of suspicion.

"Two wonderful years," I said, lying through my teeth.

"Okay then, follow me. He's just this way."

Sabrina remained in the waiting room while I followed the doctor down a hallway to a room where Hudson was lying on a bed. He was awake and smiled weakly as he saw me enter. "Mr. Beck your 'girlfriend' is here to see you."

"My girlfriend?" he said before cottoning on. "Oh, of course, honey. How good to see you… girlfriend."

The doctor rolled his eyes and left the room with a knowing smile. I walked over to the bed and sat down in a chair. "How are you doing?"

"I feel like I've been shot in the shoulder, but apart from that not too bad," he said with a mischievous smile. "I feel better now that you're here."

"Look I owe you a huge apology. You saved my life back there, and you nearly died because of that."

Hudson shrugged like it was no big deal. "I might have been pretty out of it back there, but I seem to recall your friend saving my life too. The doctors said they can't understand how I'm alive. I should have bled out in minutes. I saw her performing magic."

"How do you know about witches?" I asked. "How do you know about magic? I wouldn't have figured that's something an outlaw biker would know about."

Hudson smiled. "Let's just say I've been around a bit."

I stared at Hudson for a moment in silence, waiting for him to elaborate a little. It was a trick I had learned in journalism school; people were uncomfortable with silence and more often than not you could coax words out of them by saying less yourself. Hudson just carried on staring back at me though, those blazing brown eyes burning into me like coals.

"You're really not going to say any more than that?" I asked him.

Hudson pushed himself up in the bed, grimacing a little as he did so. "What, and give away all my secrets?" He smiled and winked. The expression put butterflies in my stomach. "Nah, I don't think so."

I rolled my eyes, but I didn't feel overtly annoyed with the mysterious biker. "Well, uh listen, thank you for saving my life back there. It was really brave of you." I swallowed down the nerves in my throat, my mind helplessly drawing back to that moment when I had been lying on the apartment floor, the weight of Hudson's body pressing down on me.

"I was just acting on instinct. It was no big deal," he said coolly.

"Right, I'm sure getting shot at and jumping out of the path of gunfire is a regular everyday thing for someone like you. It's pretty new for me though, so thanks."

"You're welcome then. Just be careful out there. The doctors want to keep me in overnight, so I won't be able to come to your rescue for the next twenty-four hours."

I laughed and realized I was moving my fingers through my hair. I stopped myself and placed my hands flat on my thighs. "Rest assured, I am leaving things in the hands of the police now. Things have already gotten way out of hand. When people start shooting, I take that as a sign to back off. I've got a bakery to reopen and stuff to unpack, so there's plenty to keep me occupied!"

"Listen before you get off, I want to ask *you* something. Give me your number." Hudson said he was going to *ask* me something, but the way he worded it felt more like a statement.

"My number?" Suddenly I felt a bead of sweat roll down my temple. Why was it so hot in here?

"Yeah… you do have one, right? You don't strike me as one of those off the grid types." Those unwavering dark browns didn't look away from me.

"O-Of course I do," I stammered. "Why do you want my number?" I gulped, wondering why I turned into this tragic nervous caricature every time I was around him.

"I want to take you out for dinner," he said calmly. "The odds of that happening improve significantly if I have your number."

I made an awful sound in response. It's like I was laughing and drowning at the same time. Hudson's brow furrowed in amusement, and I put a hand over my mouth to stop the awful drown-laugh.

"You're funny!" I said, my cheeks burning bright red as I grabbed a pen off the side table and wrote my number on a napkin. "Were you a comedian before you were in a criminal bike gang, because boy you can really tell them!" I picked the napkin up and handed him the number, my hand trembling visibly. The last thing Hudson had said wasn't even funny; I was just an absolute mess around him.

He took the napkin with the hand not in a sling, his eyes still glistening with amusement. Just then my senses took over and I snapped back to reality.

"Hang on a second, there's still something you're not telling me—" I said. "I shouldn't have done that; give it back."

"You… you want your number back? The one you just voluntarily gave to me?" he said, confusion evident on his face.

"I mean there's still something missing," I blurted quickly. "You bikers are involved in this somehow; I just know it. The night Constance died she confronted you in the park for accosting a girl that had passed by, and hours later she was dead! That can't be a coincidence!"

Hudson stared at me; his eyes narrowed. "How do you know she confronted us?" he asked.

"That doesn't matter," I said. Why did he have to know I could see Constance's ghost? "It's clear you're still hiding something, so even if you did save my life back there it's wildly inappropriate to ask for my number. Even worse for me to give it!"

The hot outlaw biker kept on staring at me. "Here's what I know," he said calmly. "I think Nick might have had something to do with it. He was the one catcalling that girl that night, and he was the one that got the brunt of your aunt's ire. We already know he stole the drug from that pharmacy, thanks to your handy work, but I don't know why he stole it in the first place."

"Come on," I scoffed. "You guys cut your product with that stuff!" I don't know how Hudson could have the audacity to keep playing stupid. Once again though he just looked at me like I was talking another language.

"I think you've grossly overestimated what we're doing down there at the park. We sell black market medical marijuana cards."

I blinked at him. "Wait, what? You're drug dealers! You sell coke, meth, heroin!"

"You think there's a big market for that in a prim and proper town like Compass Cove? I don't know why Nick stole the fentanyl in the first place, but I can assure you it has nothing to do with our operation. I thought he was your aunt's killer, but now someone else is running around firing bullets, I'm not so sure."

"I...I should go," I said quickly. I didn't know what to believe anymore. I stood up from the chair and made my way to the door. Hudson had saved my life, yes, but I couldn't talk to him any longer. Criminal or not, I knew he was hiding something from me.

"Hey!" he called out as I left the room. "You forgot to take your number back!"

I kept on walking down the hallway, back in the direction of the waiting room.

I needed a break.

CHAPTER 22

The next few days passed without much incident. I made the decision to leave the investigating up to the police now they were involved, and I took a step back to focus on my own business. I unpacked the meager collection of things I had dragged halfway across the country with me, folded up the boxes, and put them in the attic above Constance's apartment.

Thankfully there was enough to do at the bakery to keep me distracted from the fact that someone had tried to kill me this week. There were walls to paint, surfaces to dust, and an entire kitchen that needed cleaning out from top to bottom before I could even think of reopening.

The news of me being a 'Prismatic Witch' provided fruitful too, and all the witches in my family were practically humming with excitement to talk about it at any given opportunity. Personally, I still didn't really see what the fuss was all about, but I was just happy enough I had something to take my mind off the killer still on the loose.

I had plenty of help restoring the bakery too. Zelda and Celeste had a rotating schedule of half-days at Celeste's café, which meant one of them was usually always free to give me a hand. Sabrina's schedule was a little less forgiving, but she'd been stopping over in the evenings to help out. In fact, it seemed the bakery had become a de facto evening hangout for everyone in the group. I wasn't complaining; it was nice to have friends and family I could see every day. This new life was certainly a lot less isolating than my old one.

Once the majority of the refurbishments and cleaning was out of the way I had various administrative tasks to see to, ones that mostly involved mountains of arduous paperwork, unforgiving and relentlessly dull. I made an effort to get it all done as soon as possible, and after a short appointment down at the town hall the bakery was officially transferred over to my name.

With the thrilling admin taken care of I spent the rest of my time practicing recipes and building a menu for the bakery. I'd already decided to keep a majority of the items from Constance's old menu, but Zelda and I also spent quite a bit of time looking through magazines and the internet for inspiration for new items too.

I have to say I was surprised how quickly my baking ability started to come on, and also how much I was enjoying it. It was very easy to lose myself in the kitchen while tinkering away with new recipes or trying 'just one more' bake to see how things turned out if I tweaked the recipe or tried another ingredient.

More often than not I would wake up and start baking straightaway, something that was quickly becoming routine for me, and I wouldn't usually stop to look at the time until Zelda or Celeste walked in at some point during the afternoon.

"Oi, Zora, it's me, Zelda!" she shouted one afternoon as she came into the kitchen. That morning had been a particularly busy one, I'd done several traybakes: cupcakes, flapjacks, and even some English scones. Every surface was packed to the brim with my various bakes from that morning. "Uh... been busy?" she asked, looking for a spot to set her bag down. She placed it on the floor behind her and grabbed a cupcake off the surface closest to her.

"I may have gotten a little carried away," I admitted. I looked around the kitchen properly for the first time that morning and realized yes—I *migh*t have gone a little overboard. "This baking stuff is more fun than I thought!"

"That's good news, considering you own a bakery." Zelda took a bite of the cupcake and looked like she needed a moment alone with it. "Sweet mother of mischief, this cupcake is amazing."

"Thanks." I grinned. "Chocolate and cookie dough. It's a thing I'm trying out."

"I want to eat this on my deathbed. In fact, I want to be buried with this. I want my future husband to be made of this stuff."

"That might be past my level of expertise. How was your morning at the café?" I asked.

"Pretty good for the most part. Celeste is in a great mood; she had that date last night and I think it went well."

"Ooh," I said, making the sound as girly as possible. "Who is the eligible bachelor?"

"I don't know. She won't tell me anything about him! She's always so tight-lipped about her love life, it's like getting blood from a stone. Sabrina on the other hand, that girl keeps talking even after you ask her to stop."

"You're pretty tight-lipped too," I observed. Zelda's cheeks flushed slightly.

"Um, says you," she said, turning it around on me. "It's not every day a hot outlaw biker jumps in front of a bullet for you." Zelda swooned and grabbed another cupcake. "I can't believe he hasn't called you yet."

"Well, I left that room looking like a complete idiot. I gave him my number then told him to give it back. He probably picked up on the red flags and decided to toss it in the trash."

"You do give off a special brand of crazy," Zelda remarked. "You never know though; he might be one of those guys that digs that type of thing. What are you going to do with all these bakes? There's way too many here for us to polish off tonight, and to be honest, I think I need to slow down. I've already piled on several pounds since you moved here and started baking… not that I'm complaining."

"I think I'm going to take some of it down to the local food shelter.

CAKES TO DIE FOR

I looked it up and apparently there's one on the way to the car rental place. The car is due back today, so that's fun. I'll have to try and buy a cheap replacement."

"Or—" Constance said as her head floated through the countertop. Both Zelda and I jumped out of our skin and cursed her sudden appearance.

Zelda's cupcake flew out of her hand as she jumped. "Flipping heck, Constance, will you stop that!"

I closed my eyes and stilled my own breath. "What she said," I huffed. "Use the door."

"Eh, doors are for the losers left alive. The dead make grand entrances. Get used to it!" she said, spinning up through the rest of the counter, her arms held wide in dramatic flourish. "Anyway, I was going to say—just use the van. It's parked in the garage in the back alley."

"Wait, you still have that thing?" Zelda asked. "I thought you sold it."

"Nope. I just never used it." Constance looked at me and lowered her voice. "I'm a bit of a nervous driver!"

"Well that's awesome news—the van, not you being a nervous driver. Let's check it out."

"Keys are on the wall behind you; follow me!" Constance said, and zipped out the back.

Zelda and I followed her outside, around the corner to a locked garage door. Constance pointed out the right key and I unlocked the corrugated metal door.

"You're going to love it," Zelda said, smirking.

"Why do I feel like I'm on the receiving end of a bad joke here…" I said warily. I lifted up the metal garage door and immediately understood why. "Ah, I see. It's… hideous."

"Um, don't you talk about Helen that way!" Constance said.

"Helen, really? You called your van Helen?" I asked.

"She's beautiful!" Constance said defensively. "Beautiful enough to launch a thousand ships!"

'Helen' was certainly a sight alright. She was bright pink with a giant cupcake mounted to the roof, the sides of the van decorated in stars and cakes.

"It looks like a unicorn was stabbed in the stomach and threw up everywhere," I said dryly.

"Oh, leave Helen alone," Constance sighed. "She's basically brand-new and she'll treat you well. It's good for the business image too. Once people see you driving her around town, they'll know the bakery is up and running again!"

I tilted my head at her point. There was no denying it; even a blind person couldn't miss this thing. Garish was an understatement.

"You know what? A ride is a ride, and I'm not going to turn my nose up at a free van. Thank you, Constance."

"You're welcome. I would have mentioned it earlier, but I was waiting to see if you stuck around first. I've been watching you in the kitchen over the past few days and you've definitely earned your stripes."

"Well shucks, you're going to make me blush. What do you say, Zelda, should we take the van out for a spin? I'm going to need a ride back from the rental place anyway. Maybe I can drive the car and you can follow me in the van."

"Wait, you want me to drive that thing?" Zelda said, her eyes growing wide. "But people will see me, people that live in this town. Why don't I take the rental?"

"Because you're not on the insurance, and I can't afford to ding it right at the last minute. I moved that thing all the way across the country without incident; I'll do the last few blocks by myself just to make sure!" I said.

"Fine," Zelda groaned. "But you drive the van on the way back. I'm going to have to leave town if too many people see me in that thing."

Fortunately, I managed to return the rental car without incident, and I also got back my security deposit with no deductions. Zelda and I dropped off my baking at the food shelter, where the delivery was met with much delight from the woman working there.

After that, we headed back to the bakery to get a couple more things ready. It looked like we were going to have everything ready for Monday morning to finally reopen, but we still had a weekend of hard work ahead of us. I still hadn't sorted out an extra set of hands to help me out with the bakery yet; the cost of refurbishing the bakery had cost a little more than anticipated, so we'd have to be open for a few weeks first before I could afford to take someone else on.

It meant the first couple of weeks were probably going to be more stressful than necessary, but Zelda and Celeste had already reworked some hours at the café so they could help me out, and Sabrina had also roped one of her friends into helping too.

Somehow everything was starting to come together. It was surprising, but... it almost looked like we were going to pull this off.

As Zelda and I walked into the bakery I heard the phone ringing in the back. I ran into the kitchen and answered the phone.

"You need to come and pick up Rowdy," a familiar voice said down the line.

"I, what now?" I said, utterly perplexed. "Who is this?"

"It's Marjorie, you pea-brain! Now come and pick up Rowdy. If you're reopening your tragic little shop next week, it's your turn to have him. I'm closing in twenty minutes, so come and get him!" Without giving me another chance to find out what was going on Marjorie hung up.

"Who was that?" Zelda asked as she walked into the kitchen.

"Marjorie, she said something about picking up Rowdy?"

Zelda's eyes went wide in recognition. "Oh fiddlesticks, I completely forgot about Rowdy!"

I looked around the kitchen at no one in particular, pretending I was sharing my bafflement with someone else. "Uh, care to explain?"

"Right, I forget you don't know this stuff. It's weird but it kind of feels like you've been here forever, even though it's only been like a week, I—"

"Zelda," I said, pulling her back on track.

"Rowdy is this big fiberglass charity box, in the shape of a golden retriever."

"I do recall seeing that in Marjorie's bakery. Why in the name of Hulk Hogan would I take that off her?" I asked, still not getting it.

"Rowdy is like this good luck talisman. All the kitchen witches with businesses share him, passing him around once a month. I can't remember how it got started, but it's ingrained now, and we all take it seriously. There's also another part to the tradition that Rowdy is given to a food establishment owned by a witch whenever one opens in town. The last place that opened up didn't want to be involved, and they closed down in a month."

I laughed. "What a silly little tradition." I looked at Zelda, expecting her to laugh back, but the look on her face told me she was completely in on this. "Oh, you're like… part of this too, eh?"

"Celeste and I had him last month, sales were up 5%! I'm telling you, Zora, we cannot open without Rowdy."

"Well, I guess I should go and get him before Marjorie closes her— oh for the love of…" I snatched paperwork off the side that I'd forgotten to take to the town hall.

"What's wrong?" Zelda asked.

"I must have left one of the sheets here by mistake. This needed to be at the town hall today. I'll have to run it over now!"

"Uh, the town hall closed an hour ago, dude," Zelda said. "But if you hurry you can run it down to the police station and give it in there."

"That's an option?" I asked.

"Yeah, they've got a small filing desk at the station. I think Linda has a poker night with the girls from the town hall."

"There's no way I can get to the station and back to Marjorie's in time to pick up this stupid dog statue," I said, feeling myself begin to panic.

"Uh, he's not stupid, and don't incur the wrath of Rowdy! Why don't you run down to the station and drop me off at Marjorie's on the way? I'll stall to keep her open and you can pick me and Rowdy up on the way back," Zelda suggested.

"You'd really do that?" I asked. "I thought you were terrified of Marjorie?"

Zelda shrugged. "What are little sisters for? Come on, let's go!"

CHAPTER 23

It wasn't exactly the way I wanted to end the week, but with little other choice Zelda and I barreled across town in my bright pink cupcake van as we tried to do the impossible. I dropped Zelda off at Marjorie's, then I sped to the police station, promising I'd be back as quick as possible to pick up Zelda and this stupid dog thing.

Or not stupid, whatever. Don't curse me, Rowdy, oh great and benevolent god of the bakeries.

A few minutes later I brought the cupcake van to a screeching halt in the parking lot of the police station. I jumped out and ran up to the automatic glass doors of the station, dancing on my tiptoes as I waited for them to slide open. As soon as I could fit through the widening crack I burst inside and slammed my forgotten form down on the counter.

"I need you to take this for me!" I said to Linda. "It was supposed to go to the town hall today!"

"Well, well, well," Linda said slowly, spinning around on her office chair as she turned to face me. "Look who came crawling back."

"What's that supposed to mean?" I asked.

"Nothing," she said, a wide grin cracking over her face. "I've just always wanted to say that. What do we have here?" Linda pulled the form towards her and inspected it. "Ah, yeah. I can help you out with that, but first—"

"I know the spiel, just give me the clue already."

"Now that's what I like to hear!" she said, a finger raised triumphantly in the air. Linda looked down at the crossword puzzle in front of her. "A short conversation, eight letters."

"Impossible," I answered.

"No... too many letters," Linda said. "Also, that doesn't make sense. You're losing your touch, Wick!"

"I was joking. Like... a short conversation in this town seems *impossible*." It seemed there were strings involved everywhere I went in Compass Cove.

Linda didn't even crack a smile. "You know civility costs nothing."

"Lighten up, Linda." I looked around the room as I tried to think up the answer. After a moment it came to me. "Exchange!"

This time a slow smile did spread over Linda's face, and she nodded while writing out the letters. "I knew you still had it, Wick! Consider your favor done. I'll pass this over to Joan tonight, we're doing poker at her house. I'd invite you, but we play seriously, and you don't strike me as the card type."

"I like greeting cards?" I joked.

"That's what I thought," Linda replied, and she eyed the form. "A P36-J, eh?" she said. "What's that for exactly?"

"A very dry and very boring piece of documentation to officiate a request to transfer title deeds for commercial property intended for the purposes of food and/or drinks service," I said in one very long breath.

"Is that so?" Linda raised one brow, seemingly surprised I'd rattled all that off from memory. "Well, I'll take your word for it. Joan at the town hall will know what to do with it. You know I'm kind of excited the bakery is opening up again. Are you a good baker? I mean of course you are; it probably runs in the family, right?"

"You might not believe me, but a month ago I could barely boil water. My skills have come on very quickly since moving here though."

"Oh, I imagine they have. Well I'm very much looking forward to checking the place out. I used to live for Constance's cupcakes in the morning. There are other bakeries in town, of course, but none of them quite scratch the itch from Constance's baking. You know, I'm old enough to remember when Constance took over that place from Millicent. Millicent was a darn fine baker too, of course. Taught Constance everything she knew. A lot of people weren't happy when Constance took over, they thought no one would replace Millicent Slade, but they sure came around!"

"Slade?" I asked, the name catching my attention. "Like, Marjorie Slade?"

"One and the same." Linda picked up her coffee cup and took a swig. "Marjorie of course has her own place over on Main Street. A little bit sweet for my liking; she never did quite bake like her mama."

"Huh..." So that was who Constance inherited the bakery from. Marjorie's mother. *Interesting.*

"Well, good doing business with you again, Wick. By the way, how have you been holding up? I heard you nearly lost your life earlier this week. Would have been curtains were it not for that dark-eyed Hudson, huh?"

"His eyes *are* dark, aren't they," I remarked. "I was lucky he showed up, though to be honest I'm still not sure what he was doing there."

"Hmm," Linda said. "He was in here before actually. I called him to collect the belongings of the recently deceased Nick Largo." Linda held up a plastic bag with some things in it. "He didn't want them."

"Huh. Didn't he have any next of kin?"

"Not in the state. I thought Hudson might be able to contact them and pass the things on, but he said he didn't know of anybody." Linda set the bag down and I looked at the scant contents. A wallet, a few gold chains, some change, and a gold signet ring. I stared at the ring for a moment, and then crouched down to get a closer look.

"Huh," I said, wondering why the ring looked familiar. It had a heart pressed into the flat gold top.

"What?" Linda said. "Something you recognize?"

"This ring, I've seen it somewhere before, but I can't place where. Can I have a look at it?"

"Be my guest," Linda said. She pulled the ring out and handed it to me. That's when I recognized it.

"You know it's funny, Hudson was interested in that ring too," Linda said. "As soon as he saw that thing he left in a hurry. You've seen it before too?"

I turned the ring over, and under the signet I saw an inscription on the metal: *To Nick, with all my love – MS.* Slowly I looked up, the pieces all beginning to fall together in my head. "Oh my god, I think I know who—"

Suddenly my phone started ringing. I dropped the signet and took the call; it was an unknown number.

"Where are you?" Hudson asked, his breath racing down the line.

"I'm at the police station, why?"

"I just stopped off at the bakery to check in on you. I got a terrible feeling something is wrong. Where are you, I think I might have an—"

"Oh no," I said suddenly, realizing something even more terrible. "I have to go. It's Zelda, she's in danger!"

Without another word I ended the call and ran out of the station to the cupcake van. I had to be quick. If I didn't act fast my sister would die.

CHAPTER 24

I pulled up outside Marjorie Slade's bakery and ran to the door with my wand ready. The front door was locked, but I focused on *helping hand* and opened the thing pretty much straight away. Inside, the bakery was dark and quiet, my sneakers squeaking on the tiles underfoot.

Immediately I stopped and became aware of my noisy breath and heart thumping in my chest. I couldn't explain how, but a tension in the air told me I had to be careful.

"Marjorie, it's Zora!" I shouted. "Zora Wick! I know you're in here somewhere!" Very quietly I paced to the back of the shop, ducking under the counter as I did so. Over on the counter I saw the plastic golden retriever money box that Zelda had come here to collect. Only now did I realize it was bait, intended to get *me* over here so Marjorie could kill me.

"I've figured everything out!" I said. "I mean… the puzzle pieces all seem to point to you, though I profess I don't quite understand all of it yet." Tentatively I pushed open the door that led into the kitchen and found that was dark too. I recalled the *light* cantrip, and a thin beam of light illuminated from the tip of my wand, casting eerie shadows all across the kitchen.

The air was sweet with the scent of sugar and flour. A faucet was dripping somewhere across the room. In front of me I saw stairs leading up into more darkness.

The revelation came to me as soon as I learned Marjorie's mother was the one that used to own the bakery, but it was driven home when I found the signet ring in Nick's belongings. Signed by MS, unmistakably *Marjorie Slade*. I'd seen one other person with the ring—Colin from the pharmacy.

"Let's end this now; no one else has to die," I shouted up the stairs. Magic crackled on my fingertips. They were up there; I just knew it. I put my foot upon the first step, and it creaked. Pulling back, I kicked off my shoes and took the stairs in just my socks, gliding silently up into the darkness, my heart beating in my temples.

The motive seemed simple enough. Marjorie wanted her mother's bakery, but Constance got it, probably because she was the better baker. Sabrina said witches passed things on to the best suitor, not someone necessarily related to them. Marjorie obviously couldn't stand that.

But it was the rings that tied the *how* together. Marjorie was obviously a woman with multiple men on the go. A ring for Nick, that scumbag down at the park, and a ring for Colin, the pharmacist at the drug store. She used Colin to get knowledge of the hospital pharmacy layout—I doubted he was in on it—and Nick was her tool to get the deadly drug she wanted.

Nick even froze the lock using ice spray. Glancing to my left I saw a shelf of identical ice spray tins, the same ones Marjorie used for her impressive chocolate sculpture displays.

Reaching the top of the stairs I dimmed my wand and saw faint light. Peeking around the corner I saw a messy living room and a small TV in the corner, the static on its screen casting bright light across the floor.

Great, as if this wasn't creepy enough already, I thought to myself.

"Listen," I said, making my voice clear. At this point it was obvious Marjorie wasn't coming out with her hands up, which meant I had to talk her down or fight her down. I just had to find her first. "Let's just talk about this like reasonable adults. I can leave town. I can give you the bakery."

"Ha!" a voice came from somewhere in the darkness. Got her. "It's too late for that now, Wick! Don't you see that?!"

Coming around the corner I finally saw them. Marjorie was standing in the kitchen, Zelda tied to a chair in front of her. Zelda was bound and gagged. I caught her eye and she nodded, indicating she was unharmed. Marjorie had a wand pointed right at Zelda's head.

"I see something alright," I said. "Mind explaining what's going on here?"

"Oh, just another case of Marjorie messing up as usual!" Marjorie said, a shrill and unnerving cackle following the words.

"Let's just relax," I said, stepping forward with my hands held up.

"Take one more step and I turn her brains into meat confetti."

Gross. "Okay, okay. Let's take a deep breath. We both know I'm the one you wanted here, so just let Zelda go and this can all be over with."

Marjorie cackled again and shook her head. "Put the wand down. Put it down, now!" I did as she said, throwing the wand across the room.

"It's down, okay? Now just let Zelda go."

"You don't know what it was like," Marjorie said. "Living in her shadow. Mother, the *great Millicent Slade!* I could never bake like her; all I wanted to do was impress her. I tried, I tried hard. I was always good at sculpture, but that was a waste of time in her eyes. They all loved her, but they never saw how she belittled me, how she treated me!"

"It must have been hard," I said, my eyes locked on the wand in Marjorie's hand.

"That's not even the tip of the iceberg. Still... she learned her lesson. Terrible back pain in her later years, prescribed fentanyl to deal with it. One day I made sure she got an accidental triple dose, but whoopsie, little did I know she'd left the bakery to Constance. Of course she did! Constance the darling, everyone loved her!"

"And years later you killed Constance in almost the exact same manner, but it took you time to get your hands on more fentanyl. Sinking your claws into a pharmacist and a criminal sure made short work of that though."

Marjorie laughed coldly. "Nick acted so tough, but he was easy to wrap around my finger. A scared little boy, pretending to be a man. Colin was easy. He was lonely, nothing difficult."

"But why kill Nick?" I asked.

"Because of you. You were starting to close in on him. He was the only one who knew I killed Constance that night. He got me the fentanyl, he knew I was going to go and see her. It wouldn't be long until he talked, so I got to him first, as much as it broke my heart."

"That's why your eyes were all red the morning after. You'd been crying."

She shrugged indifferently. "I've got to look after myself. No more mistakes. That means the two of you have to die. You especially. I would have gotten you at Nick's apartment if it wasn't for that white knight of yours."

"That was you?" I said in amazement. "But you were so fast, how could you—" I paused, and that was when I remembered Marjorie saying she had been a track and field star back in her youth. "The running."

"That's right!" she cackled. "I might have a bit more around the midriff now, but I can still move with the best of them. Anyway, I think we're done now, Miss Wick. You figured it all out, congratulations, but I'm afraid you have no one to share your story with."

In the darkness I suddenly heard a click. Marjorie lifted her other arm and pointed the pistol at me. "Oh… bugger," I groaned.

"Ha! Forgot about the gun, didn't you? Don't worry. I'll be pleasant and kill you both at the same time. You with the gun, Zelda here with the wand. No sense in drawing things out any longer than necessary."

In that instant I focused all my energy on blasting that wand out of her hand. I didn't care about saving myself. All that mattered was smashing the wand away from Zelda's head and giving her a chance to break free. I didn't have a wand, but by all accounts I didn't need one. As long as I really focused, I could do this.

I imagined an anvil floating in the air above Marjorie's wand arm and got ready to drop it at the right moment. *God, I hope this works.*

"Farewell, Wick sisters. You've been a real pain in my—"

"Zelda, run!" I shouted. At that moment I willed my spell into action and watched as Marjorie's arm slammed down to her waist and her wand clattered across the floor. She cried out in pain and I jerked my head to the side, pulling Zelda across the apartment with more magic, sending her whizzing past me, still tied to her chair.

"My arm! You broke my arm, you psychotic little tripe!" Marjorie roared. She straightened back up, pointed the gun at me, and went to pull the trigger when a huge figure crashed through the window behind her. Two black boots smashed into her back and sent her to the floor.

Hudson landed on Marjorie with his knee digging into her back. He pulled a pair of handcuffs out of nowhere and slapped them around her wrists. "Marjorie Slade, I'm arresting you under suspicion of murdering Constance Wick and Nick Largo! Anything you say can and will be used against you in a court of law!"

I stood there with my mouth flapping open and closed, unable to process what I was seeing. "Hudson, is a—Hudson is a—he's a—"

"He's a cop, Zora!" Zelda cried out from behind me. "Now get me out of this chair already; these binds are killing me!"

I hurried over to my sister, untied her from the overturned chair and helped her to her feet. With Marjorie cuffed, Hudson came over to us and grinned. "Great work, Miss Wick. I think it's safe to say we can draw a line under this one."

"You're a cop!" I repeated in amazement. It turned out my outlaw biker wasn't an outlaw after all.

Hudson just grinned and winked at me. "Happy now?" he asked. "You've finally figured out my secret."

"And solved Constance's murder!" Zelda said.

"Not bad for your first week in town," Hudson said, and clasped his hand on my shoulder. "Come on, let's get you guys outside and have the paramedics look you over."

And with that, the mystery came to an end. Hudson escorted us out of the building with Marjorie in tow, handcuffed to prevent her from doing any further damage.

We'd caught the killer and solved Constance's murder… but there were still questions I didn't have answers to.

CHAPTER 25

ONE WEEK LATER

"To a successful first week," I said to Zelda, holding up a cup of tea and toasting in jest. We clinked our cups together and collapsed onto the sofa in my apartment. The week had been hectic, the café opening on Monday to a line that went around the block.

After helping to solve Constance's death and capturing Marjorie, I had somehow become a celebrity in town overnight. A front-page news article went out on Monday, and a picture of my face was right underneath the headline, for all the town to see: *Local Woman Uncovers Mystery Murder Poison Plot!*

After the paper went out, the rest of the week was chaos. The article told people all about Marjorie's crimes, and also advertised for free that Constance's bakery was opening up again, under my ownership. We'd basically been given front-page advertising for free, and Constance was delighted.

"Talk about a trial by fire!" she said as she floated up through the apartment floor. Zelda and I were too tired to be scared. "Do you know how much money you took this week? We couldn't have asked for a better start!"

"You need to hire someone, pronto," Zelda groaned. "I can't carry on with two jobs for much longer. Celeste's café was already enough!"

I nodded in agreement. "I'll sort that out next week. I just have to make it through the weekend alive first." Thankfully Zelda had roped a couple of her witch friends into helping us out this weekend, so things might feel a little easier.

"I'm going home to sleep for like thirty hours," Zelda said. "Don't attempt to contact me. I will kill the first person that wakes me up."

"Message received loud and clear!" I chuckled as Zelda shuffled down the stairs and left. Hermes looked up at me from the windowsill, opening one sleepy eye. "Well haven't you had an eventful two weeks."

"That's putting it lightly," I said. "Hopefully things will settle down a little bit now. I can focus on running the bakery and it'll all be smooth sailing from here." Hermes stood up, stretched, and then cackled. "What's funny?" I asked.

"Oh, I'm sure it's all going to be a walk in the park from this point."

"I'm detecting not-so-subtle tones of sarcasm."

Hermes jumped down from his seat, walked over to me, and hopped onto the couch. "So, you're a Prismatic Witch," he remarked.

"Yeah?"

"Did you think that title was just for fun? That role comes with responsibility. I've been reading about Prismatic Witches; trouble follows them like stink on a wet dog."

I gulped. "What does that mean?"

Hermes shrugged. It was unusual to see a cat shrug, even a talking one. "Oh, you'll see. It won't be long before the witches around here start crawling out of the woodwork. Everyone will want a piece of you."

"Great," I said. "As if I wasn't busy enough already."

"Hey, the rest of the evening is yours! You've earned it. Let's sit back, watch some old movies, and relax. Take the phone off the hook and lock the door."

"Now there's a plan I can get behind—" I began, interrupted as the doorbell rang downstairs. "I better get that. Then the relaxing begins!"

"Sure, sure," Hermes said with a roll of his eyes.

I made my way downstairs, and as I made my way into the bakery, I saw the person standing on the other side of the glass door. I unlocked it and pulled the door open. "Hudson," I said in disbelief. I hadn't seen him since the incident at Marjorie's. "What are you doing here?"

"I realized I never gave you this back," he said, handing me a piece of paper. I took it and realized it was the napkin I had given him at the hospital. It still had my number on it.

"Very funny," I said, rolling my eyes. I passed it back to him. "You can keep it. I'd kind of given up on you calling me anyway."

"I was a little busy trying to catch a murderer," he smiled, "and if you cast your mind back to last week, I did."

"I remember. You saved my life. I guess that puts you in the lead again." Hudson chuckled. "I can't believe you're a cop, I mean—now that I think about it, it makes sense in retrospect, but it really took me by surprise."

"I've been working undercover here for a year. Nick Largo was my target. He was suspected to be connected to some larger things; I can't go into much more detail."

I held my hands up as if it was spooky. "Serious undercover stuff. I get it. Maybe you can clue me on in this though; how did you come crashing through that window just in time? How did you even know I was up there? How did you figure it out?"

"When I saw that signet ring in Nick's things, I found the inscription. I didn't know who *MS* was, but I remembered that pharmacist having the same ring. That immediately put alarm bells in my mind."

"You never saw Nick wear the ring before that?" I asked.

Hudson shook his head. "Nope. He wore it on a chain around his neck. I never even saw the thing before that. I rushed to the drug store and asked Colin who gave him the ring. I had no idea who Marjorie Slade was, but he told me she ran a bakery on Main Street. When I drove back there, I saw your van pulled up outside and knew there must have been trouble."

I mean the answer made sense enough, but it still didn't explain how Hudson had come swinging down through the right window, right at the exact time he needed to. "I..." I began.

"You still have questions," he said, his eyes gleaming at me.

"Uh, yeah. Like, what kind of cop are you? That was some real superhero stuff you pulled off, and what about your shoulder? Three days before the incident your arm was in a cast, and then you're swinging around on rappel ropes like some Hollywood action hero?"

Hudson looked up and down the empty street behind him and looked back at me. He reached into his jacket pocket and pulled out a black business card. I took it and read it.

Hudson Beck. Agent 417. Above that in large white letters was the word *M.A.G.E.*

"MAGE? What is MAGE?" I asked.

"Magical Agency for General Enigmas. We're a branch of the government network that doesn't exist. Memorize that number, the card will destroy itself in ten seconds."

"Right," I laughed. "And I bet you've got a pen in your pocket that will erase my memory—ah!" The card suddenly burst into flames, and I dropped it to the ground, watching in bewilderment as it turned to ash. "What the heck?!"

"I warned you," he said with a smile. "417. That's me. If you ever need me, then just call."

"Your phone number is 417? Three digits?" Hudson nodded as though that was completely normal. "If this is all so secretive then why are you telling me all about it?" I asked.

"I'm glad you asked. You see, I've heard some rumors about you, Zora Wick. It's not every day a Prismatic Witch comes into town. Your kind are rare, and I expect we're going to be working with each other quite a bit more."

"So, this was a business call," I said. I don't know why, but I found my heart sinking in my chest slightly. Even though I knew a little more about Hudson now, it felt like every answer brought more questions. Who was this man of mystery?

"Yes, and I should probably make this clear now. As a field agent

I'm not supposed to have intimate relationships with those I work with, and in your new capacity we are now colleagues of sorts."

"Right, of course—" I said, staring down at the ground and wondering why I imagined even for a moment that anything could happen between a girl like me and a guy like Hudson. Then something completely unexpected happened. Hudson stepped forward and kissed me.

His hands were on my hips, his lips pressed against mine. For a few seconds it was just the two of us, the world spinning around me, my head swimming from the strange tide of emotions swirling through me. He pulled away and I was staring at him.

"What…" I said, unable to muster anything else. There was a huge goofy smile on my face. "But I thought you just said—"

Hudson shrugged. "Eh, what are rules for if not to be broken? Goodbye, Zora Wick. See you around." With that, Hudson stepped back onto the sidewalk, bowed his head slightly, and wandered off into the night. I locked the door, headed back upstairs to the apartment, feeling like I was floating the whole way.

"Well, don't you look happy!" Hermes remarked. "Who was at the door?"

"Oh… no one," I said, curling up on the couch next to him and smiling to myself. "Come on, let's watch a film, kitty."

CLICK HERE to read Book 2: A Brunch With Death.

THANKS FOR READING

Thanks for reading, I hope you enjoyed the book.

It would really help me out if you could leave an honest review with your thoughts and rating on Amazon.

Every bit of feedback helps!

ALSO BY MARA WEBB

~ Ongoing ~

Hallow Haven Witch Mysteries

An English Enchantment

Compass Cove Cozy Mysteries

~ Completed ~

Wicked Witches of Pendle Island

Wildes Witches Mysteries

Raven Bay Mysteries

Wicked Witches of Vanish Valley

MAILING LIST

Want to be notified when I release my latest book? Join my mailing list. It's for new releases only. No spam:

Click here to join!

I'll also send you a free 120,000 word book as a thank you for signing up.

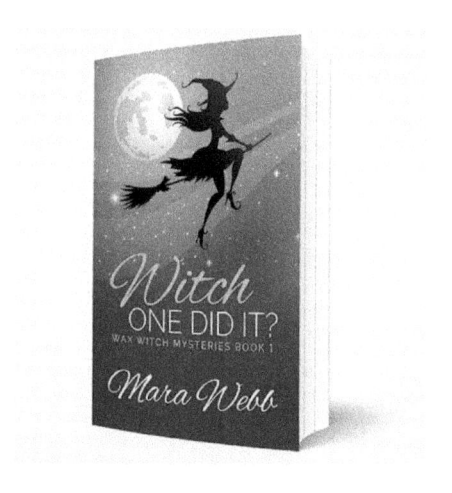

marawebbauthor.com

amazon.com/-/e/B081X754NL
facebook.com/marawebbauthor
twitter.com/marawebbauthor
bookbub.com/authors/mara-webb